D0974512

MAGGIE SHAYNE

It was a sleepless night spent caring for a sick baby that jump-started *New York Times* bestselling author Maggie Shayne's writing career.

A voracious reader and prolific writer from childhood, Maggie found herself without a book to read while coddling her colicky child. So she began spinning a tale of her own. Now the author of more than forty novels, Maggie has honed her lyrical prose and made a name for herself on the *New York Times, USA TODAY,* Amazon.com, B.Dalton, Booksense, Ingram's, Barnes & Noble and Waldenbooks bestseller lists.

Maggie is also the winner of numerous awards, including two *RT Book Reviews* Career Achievement Awards, a National Readers Choice Award and the coveted RITA® Award.

MAUREEN CHILD

is a California native, who loves to travel. Every chance they get, she and her husband are taking off on another research trip. The author of more than sixty books, Maureen loves a happy ending and still swears that she has the best job in the world. She lives in Southern California with her husband, two children and a golden retriever with delusions of grandeur. Visit Maureen's website at www.maureenchild.com.

MAGGIE SHAYNE

&

MAUREEN CHILD

VACATION WITH A VAMPIRE...
and Other Immortals

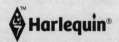

Harlequin®

TORONTO NEW YORK LONDON
AMSTERDAM PARIS SYDNEY HAMBURG
STOCKHOLM ATHENS TOKYO MILAN MADRID
PRAGUE WARSAW BUDAPEST AUCKLAND

ISBN-13: 978-0-373-61862-0

VACATION WITH A VAMPIRE...
AND OTHER IMMORTALS

Recycling programs
for this product may
not exist in your area.

Copyright © 2011 by Harlequin Books S.A.

The publisher acknowledges the copyright holders
of the individual works as follows:

VAMPIRES IN PARADISE
Copyright © 2011 by Margaret Benson

IMMORTAL
Copyright © 2011 by Maureen Child

This edition published by arrangement with Harlequin Books S.A.

For questions and comments about the quality of this book
please contact us at Customer_eCare@Harlequin.ca.

® and TM are trademarks of the publisher. Trademarks indicated with
® are registered in the United States Patent and Trademark Office, the
Canadian Trade Marks Office and in other countries.

www.Harlequin.com

Printed in U.S.A.

CONTENTS

VAMPIRES IN PARADISE

Maggie Shayne

Dear Reader,

"Vampires in Paradise" is a story that stands alone. I deliberately set it on a deserted island so that you could enjoy it whether or not you had ever read another of my vampire stories.

That said, you probably ought to know that there have been twenty. That includes several novellas, one online read and one novel that hasn't yet been released. This year's titles are *Twilight Prophecy,* which came out in mid-April, and *Twilight Fulfilled,* which will be released toward the end of September.

I've been writing vampires since 1993's *Twilight Phantasies* for Silhouette Shadows, you see. And thanks to modern technology, you can now find nearly every book in my "Wings in the Night" backlist at Harlequin.com and in Kindle and Nookbook formats. So now there's just no possible excuse not to read them all, right?

Either way, I really hope you enjoy "Vampires in Paradise."

Best,

Maggie Shayne

Chapter 1

"I'm sorry, Anna, but there is no cure."

Anna Seville sat in a chair facing her doctor and friend, Mary St. Augustine, and waited for the punch line. But there wasn't one. Mary was known for her stoic disposition. In fact, since high school, Anna had never seen Mary cry. But her eyes were welling with tears now, and that only added credence to the impossible pronouncement. But all Anna's brain kept repeating was that *this just couldn't be right*.

"There's a mistake somewhere, Mary, there has to be. I'm not...I can't be...dying." Saying the word, though it had emerged only as a whisper, seemed to make it more real. Dying. Ending. Leaving. Her life was *over.*

Suddenly Anna felt cold, and her focus seemed to turn inward, searching for logic or reason somewhere. Anywhere. But Mary's words had just taken it all away.

So she sought for rational reasons why it couldn't possibly be true. "I haven't even been all that sick. Just...you know, tired. Worn out. Lethargic."

"I know. That's one of the main symptoms of this condition."

"But I don't have a *condition.* I've been fine my whole life, and now you're telling I was born with some sort of flaw that—"

"If you'd come to me sooner, I'd have told you sooner. But you've spent your whole adult life dodging health care at every possible opportunity."

"Yeah, and look what happens the first time I give in to the nagging and come in for a checkup. A death sentence."

Mary lowered her head. "Maybe on some level you knew."

Anna sighed. "My mom did, I think. Probably why she was always running me to doctors and being so overprotective when I was a kid. God, why didn't she tell me?"

"I imagine she intended to, when she thought you were old enough. It's not as if she planned to have a heart attack at thirty-nine."

And now it didn't look as if her eldest daughter would outlive her by much, Anna thought sadly.

"What is it, Mary? What's killing me?" she asked, ready, she thought, to hear the truth.

Mary shook her head. "You were born with a rare blood antigen known as Belladonna. It was never detected until now because you've never been a donor or needed a transfusion, or had any major surgeries."

"And if I had been?" Anna asked, instantly ready to blame herself for not being generous and donating blood like any decent citizen would do. She'd always meant to, she'd just been so busy with other things. Her job and all her causes, and her sister's, Lauren's, kids—until they'd turned on her, anyway.

After their mother had died unexpectedly, Anna had become Lauren's caretaker. Her enabler, actually. Lauren had drifted into addiction— prescription drugs, mostly, at the beginning, but that soon degenerated into anything she could get her hands on. She'd had two babies in a row, Nate and Cindi, with no father in sight for either of them. And hell, someone had to make sure the kids had a roof over their heads.

Anna realized that Mary had been talking and she'd been oblivious. She fixed her eyes on her friend and said, "Sorry, I drifted. Would you start over?"

Mary nodded. "The Belladonna antigen is rare. Few people have it. Those who do tend to bleed very easily. Almost like a hemophiliac would. Your mother probably knew this, and that's why she was so worried about every little cut and scrape you got as a kid."

"Makes sense. Okay, what else? Has anyone ever…beaten this?"

Mary shook her head. "Everyone with this condition experiences the same symptoms you've been describing. Onset occurs in the mid-thirties, on average."

She was speaking in sound bites, Anna realized. Uttering a fact or two, then pausing to be sure Anna had heard and understood before moving on. She was watching Anna's face now, waiting for a signal.

"Okay. So far I'm just like everyone else who has this…condition. So what happens next?" She blinked, then focused on Mary's eyes. "Tell me the truth. How bad will it be?"

"It's a very easy, gentle process, Anna. And that's the truth. There's no pain. You'll just keep feeling weaker, more lethargic. You'll begin sleeping more and more. Patients often find that daylight becomes harsh and unbearable, so they tend to become a bit nocturnal toward the end. Eventually you'll just fall asleep and won't wake up again."

Anna nodded slowly.

"Anna, it's usually less than a year from the onset of symptoms to the end. And you've been feeling them for…what? A couple of months now?"

She thought back. "It's hard to say. It was so subtle at first, you know? I just thought I needed iron or more vitamins or something. It's been three months since they got to the point where I was worried." She thinned her lips. "But I knew you'd ask, so I got out my journal. And the first time I made a note about feeling as if I were tiring more easily than I should was six months before that."

Mary's eyes widened just a little. "And yet you didn't come in sooner?"

"I kept hoping it would pass on its own." Anna

held Mary's eyes. "And you said it wouldn't have made any difference."

"It wouldn't. Just would have given you more time to—"

"Time. God, time." Suddenly she was eager to get out of the chair, get busy, get moving. If she only had three months to live... "I've got so much to get done! I'll have to put my house on the market, make arrangements for the money to go to Nate and Cindi—and the car, what am I going to do about the car?" She was moving around Mary's office as she spoke, looking for her jacket, that was on a coatrack near the door. Long and deep green, a trench-style coat for the spring rains. "I don't even have a will. I'll need to write one immediately. Where did I put my purse? Oh, God, work. What about work? I have to help them find a replacement for me. And there's that big fundraiser we're doing for the SPCA! It's six months away, and I might not even be here to—"

"Anna."

The firm, clipped nature of Mary's tone reached her. She stopped talking, stopped moving, right there in front of the desk.

"Please sit down. Just for five more minutes. Just sit down and listen, okay?"

Frowning, Anna sat, noticing that her purse was on the floor beside her chair. How had she not seen it right there?

Mary got up and came around her desk. She pulled a vacant chair around to face Anna, then sat down, leaning forward, her arms resting on her legs. "I'm talking to you as your friend now, not as your doctor, okay?"

Anna nodded.

"This is your life we're talking about. Three months, give or take—they're all you've got left. Do you understand that?"

"Of course I do. You just told me."

"And your response was to list all the stuff you have to do for other people. Your sister turned on you when her kids were finally on their own, and you told her you wouldn't keep helping her pay her bills unless she gave up her drug habit. Hell, the kids turned on you, too, after you practically raised them and put them through college, when you refused to bail their mother out of jail last year. They haven't spoken to you since, have they?" Anna lowered her eyes, shook her head. It was true. Nate and Cindi had vowed never to speak to her again for letting their mother rot in a cell. She'd been out in a month and using again, anyway.

"You have time now," Mary went on. "And fairly decent health for a while yet, too. I'm telling you to stop thinking about everyone else and figure out what *you* want to do. What do you want to experience that you never have? How do you want to spend the last days of your life? Figure that out, Anna, and once you do, say 'to hell with everyone else.' And just go do it. They'll all figure things out when it's over."

Anna sat there, blinking. "But if I don't…take care of things, then who will?"

Mary shrugged. "Go on a dream vacation. Write a will while you're there. Pick someone you trust to name as your executor. Mail it to them, and they'll see to it that everything gets handled. They'll sell your house and give the money to whoever you name. They'll see to everything you want just the way you want it. You don't need to do it now. I can't bear to see you wasting what's left of your life taking care of everyone but yourself."

Anna lowered her head, blinking slowly. "But…that's what I've always done."

"I know it is, hon. I know. And you've earned your place in heaven—as well as the right to be just a little bit selfish now that you know your time is limited."

Anna released a pent-up breath. "I'm not sure I even know how. I don't even know what to do."

"Think on it. Don't think about death or dying, or your sister or her kids. Think about what you would do if you could do anything you wanted. Anything at all. What would it be? What would you see, where would you go, what would you wear?"

Anna nodded, her gaze again turning inward as Mary's words stirred visions and dreams she'd left along the roadsides of her life. Her short, empty life. Dreams of sailing. Of the ocean. Of tropical islands. And of a dark-eyed man who loved her with the kind of passion she'd read about in romance novels all her life. The one she'd longed for, dreamed about, fantasized, and sensed was out there…somewhere. She'd always thought he would be waiting when she got around to searching for him.

But she'd never gotten around to it, had she?

"Will you do that for me, Anna?" Mary was asking.

Anna nodded. "I…I will." She nodded harder as she got up from her chair. "Yes. Thank you, Mary. I'm going to think about this. About what you've said. About what…I…want."

Mary stood, looking at her. "Promise?"

"I promise."

Mary wrapped her in a delicate hug, and Anna knew her friend was crying, felt it in the way her body trembled ever so slightly from trying to hold it inside. "I love you, you know," Mary said, her voice deeper than before. "I love you."

"I love you, too," Anna told her. Then she broke the embrace. "I'll let you know what… what I decide."

"Thank you. I'd love that, but don't feel obligated. From this moment on, Anna, your life is about you. About you doing what *you* feel like doing. Period. Okay?"

"Okay." She stood, too, facing her friend, blinking through tears that matched the ones dampening Mary's lashes. "Thank you," she said softly.

Mary nodded and kissed her cheek.

Turning toward the office door, Anna drew a deep breath and then went through it, not looking back. She didn't slow or think or pause until she was sitting behind the wheel of her car, and about to turn the key.

But she couldn't. She looked around her at all the people passing by, and she wondered how they could all seem so…ordinary. How were they just going about their everyday lives as if the entire world hadn't just turned upside down?

She laid her head on the steering wheel and cried.

Chapter 2

Diego leaped easily from the gleaming hardwood deck of the *Santa Maria XIII* onto the pier without need of a gangplank. He didn't own a dock of his own on the mainland because it was fairly important he not show up at the same coastal port town too often. This one was in the mishmash of peninsulas and islands along the blurred edges of North and South Carolina, where it was often tough to tell which state one was technically inhabiting. He'd used it before. The closest town was Kendall, but this long public access pier was beyond the town limits, in the middle of nowhere, with nothing much to mark it besides one of the most beautiful lighthouses he'd seen. Tall, black and white, simple, but elegant and solid. It seemed as permanent as the rocky peninsula on which it stood. And far more elegant than the man-made walking path, pretty park benches and manicured flower gardens that surrounded it.

He'd tied his sailboat securely and knew she would still be there on his return. It wasn't often he ventured onto the mainland. He viewed doing so as a necessary evil, a task he performed as seldom as he possibly could—about every three months or so. And even then, only by dead of night, when he was far less likely to encounter humankind. He preferred the smell of the sea to that of their sweat and their sex and their fear of all things unknown. He preferred the innocent perfection of nature to the mistrust and cynicism of man. Part of nature…once, yes, man had been that. But he'd veered so far from natural that he no longer qualified. He was all but a machine at this point. He'd lost his connection to his mother.

They would call *him* unnatural, he supposed, but in his own mind, Diego was the most natural creature he could imagine. Not that being a vampire made him naturally good. Some of his kind were as bad as the humans were. Some were worse. Far, far worse.

He walked in silence along the pier, hating that the energy of peace, of blessed harmony, was slowly being overcome by the raucous and unnatural thoughts and emotions of the world of man. He'd tried his best to prepare for the mental onslaught, but, as usual, he'd failed.

He felt anger and rage. Couples arguing, men fighting, parents shouting at their children. He felt the despondence of the homeless and the cravings of the addicts. He felt the fear of the innocent, not yet cruel enough to hold their own among the melee. He smelled the chemicals and exhaust in the air, and he wished for nothing more than to complete his task as quickly as possible and return to his haven, where none of that existed.

And then he felt *her*.

He'd reached the landward end of the pier and stepped from it onto the little path that meandered past the lighthouse. She wasn't far from him—a few dozen meters at most—and her emotions were overwhelming her. They were mixed, but the most prominent among them was sadness. And in spite of himself, he tuned in to her above all the other noise in his mind. He focused on her and listened in, and he heard the thoughts racing around in her head.

My life is ending before it's even begun...

How can it be true? How can it be true? How can it be true?

What will happen? Is there a heaven? Do I deserve to go there?

Should I do it? Can I possibly be that selfish, even now?

What about Lauren? What about Nate and Cindi?

The kids are going to have to learn to fend for themselves, anyway. It's not as if Lauren's capable of taking care of them.

They're adults. They'll manage. God knows I did.

I deserve some happiness.

I don't have much time left.

I could just go. Just buy the boat and go...

God, it would be so beautiful. So peaceful. So restful.

How can I be so selfish?

He frowned, pulling away from her jumbled emotions and telling himself it was none of his business, anyway. Turning, he started to walk in the other direction, toward the town and the victim he would take tonight. A criminal or an abuser or a thug. No one worthy of using up this beautiful planet's precious resources. Like lancing a boil, removing one of those. He was performing a service. And he only allowed himself the pleasure a few times a year, when he came in for supplies. The rest of the time, those supplies were his sustenance. Stolen from one of the various blood banks, clinics and hospitals that were his usual sources.

He was running low on supplies out on the island. It was time to restock. And while dealing with humans and their world full of misery was something he dreaded, he had to admit that he looked forward to the taking of a live victim on these quarterly excursions. There was nothing quite like the rush of warm, living blood—not to mention the power of it.

Dying. Dying. How can I possibly be dying?

Her thoughts stopped him again, and he turned once more, gazing along the shore, spotting her. She was on the same path as he was, on one of the benches, but farther out on the long finger of the earthen pier, near the tall lighthouse at its tip. The sentinel stood impassive, as always, its black barber-pole stripe flawlessly twining upward, to the sunlike yellow glow at the top. He loved lighthouses. Perhaps because they were as close as he would get to ever seeing actual sunlight again, aside from that reflected in the mirror of the moon.

She was sitting on a stone bench, the lighthouse at her back, her gaze on the sea. He sniffed the air and caught the scent of her tears, of her skin. The soap and cologne she used, the shampoo.

He should stop right there. He should not notice anything more about her. Because what he had already noticed was tugging at him. She was dangerous.

Like Cassandra had been. Cassandra, who'd come to him at the end of her mortal life, knowing exactly what she intended. Making him fall so deeply in love with her that he would have done anything for her. Anything.

And then destroying him once she got what she wanted. When all the while, all she'd had to do was ask.

No, he wanted no part of any beautiful woman in misery. But then, just then, he caught the scent of something else about this weeping woman.

Her blood.

And it was unlike the blood of most mortals. It held the antigen that made her…a relative of his, to put it most simply. She possessed the rare Belladonna antigen. Just like Cassandra had.

Hell, she was one of the Chosen. That made her doubly dangerous to him.

Mortals with the antigen were the only ones who could ever become what he was. Vampires sensed these special humans and were compelled, often to their own detriment, to protect and watch over them. For a vampire to harm one of the Chosen was, it was said, impossible.

He'd only encountered one other. The woman who'd brought him to his knees with a heartache so crippling, he'd vowed there would never be another. And that alone made him want to leave this one to her suffering. She likely deserved it, anyway.

Again he tried to walk away, knowing now, at least, why her emotions outshouted all the other mental energies wafting on the airwaves this night.

And again his steps halted and he turned in her direction. Compelled, like a feline by the scent of catmint. Every instinct in his body was telling him to help her, to ease her pain, to go to her—while every thought in his brain told him the opposite.

He could not resist going to her. He couldn't.

Sighing, vowing that he would only speak to her briefly, be of help if he could, and that then he would leave and never so much as *think* of her again, he followed the twisting path to the bench where she sat, still weeping.

He stood over her, looking down at her. She lifted her head, sensing him there, but didn't even gasp in surprise. Her eyes narrowed. But she said nothing.

She was beautiful. Utterly beautiful. Auburn curls, wild and thick, falling over her shoulders, and huge blue eyes that seemed to reflect the soul of the sea itself. Her skin was pale already, and she had a sprinkling of freckles across the bridge of her nose, spilling just slightly onto her cheeks.

And in spite of himself, he felt her pain so sharply and so keenly it nearly brought tears to his own eyes.

"There cannot be anything so dire as to make a woman as beautiful as you are weep this bitterly."

She blinked. "I've just been told I'm dying."

"We're born dying, lady. But in truth, there's no such thing as death. We're eternal beings, whether we choose to stay or move on."

Her brows bent toward each other. "I wasn't given a choice."

"You will be. When the time comes, you will be."

Her frown deepened. "How can you know that?"

He shrugged, not telling her that despite his vow only moments ago, he would probably be the one to give her that choice. Not yet, not now. It was too soon. He could feel the life force in her and sensed there was time yet for her. But when the time of her death came, he would return and offer her the choice, or some other vampire would find her and do it. For she gave every sign of being worthy.

Though he'd thought that about Cassandra, too. Blinded by his own treacherous heart.

Not so this time. Not yet. Not if he didn't let himself be.

He would return, yes, when her time was near, and he would ask her if she wanted to live on as one of the Undead. He would offer her that option. He decided it on the spot, which was very unlike him.

She rose from the bench, her eyes staring into his as she blinked her tears away. "What should I do?"

He held her gaze, peering deeply into her eyes, slipping his will inside her mind, and finding it a beautiful place to dwell. Damn, he liked this woman. In her unguarded mind, he poked through all the litter. Obligation. Guilt. Other people's needs. More guilt. He pushed all that aside and whispered, "Let go, Anna. Let go and show me your truest heart."

As he whispered the words, he willed her to comply. He saw her eyes widen when he spoke her name, and then he felt her surrender. Her own will melted under the force of his mind. He saw her standing at the helm of a wooden sailboat. He saw her with the wind in her hair and the sea waves beneath her vessel, riding them like a triumphant Valkyrie.

"You want to sail," he said softly. "You long to be one with the sea and with the creatures who live there, and with the sky and the wind." It stunned him how much her idea of perfection matched his own. "You need to sell the house and use the money to buy the boat of your dreams."

"I do?"

"It's what you truly want." And with those words, he withdrew his will from her mind, leaving open the trail he'd blazed for her, through all the baggage and useless guilt.

"But what about my sister? What about her kids?"

He blinked at her. "Why do you cling to the need to be needed?"

"Is that what I'm doing?"

He shrugged.

Lifting a trembling hand, she touched his face, then drew her fingertips away. "You're not real, are you?"

You were put upon this planet to make the most of your life, Anna. To do so, then, cannot be deemed selfish, can it? His mind spoke directly to hers.

She was looking up at him as if he had spoken aloud, but knowing he hadn't. Her hair danced on the sea wind, almost as if reaching toward him. Her skin was pale, paler, even, than his own. And her eyes…as blue as the sea. Her beauty was beyond anything he'd ever seen.

Don't go there, he told himself. Tell her something to help her, and then go about your business and forget you ever saw her. Do it.

But as she stared at him, a smile toyed with the corners of her full, ripe lips. "I've dreamed of you, I think."

"And when was that?" he asked softly.

"All my life." Her hands rose, one touching the nape of his neck, fingers lingering there, and he felt every point of contact to the core of his being. "That you would come to me now, of all times…"

"I'm just a stranger, passing by and offering unasked-for advice."

"But you knew my name. And my deepest desires."

He should have been alarmed at having revealed so much, but he couldn't seem to drum up a hint of common sense. She was listening to him, and it was helping her. And more. He felt he was touching this woman's soul, and it was affecting him as much as it was her. Why was that? How could it be?

He whispered again to her mind, eager now to help her and then be on his way, because the feelings swirling inside him were beyond anything he understood, and he needed to be alone to figure it all out.

No loving creator would give a woman desires and then forbid her from fulfilling them. It is not selfish to wish to live your life to its fullest, no matter how long or how short it might be. To do so is sacred. It's your calling. It's why you are here. The sin would be to do anything less. I promise you that.

"Are you an angel?"

He smiled at her question. *Follow your heart,* he told her. *It is the guidance you've been given*

*all your life. It shows your true north. It leads
you true—always.*

It was a philosophy he believed in. Admittedly,
doing so had earned him the worst hurt of his
existence, but it had also led him to paradise.
The life he led now was blissful, if lonely. And
he wouldn't have found it without the heartbreak
that came before.

He felt her mind gently sliding into agreement,
felt peace settling over her like a soft, warm
blanket. Like the velvet night itself. He felt her
nodding, and even sensed relief floating into her
soul.

He had helped her. And now, he told himself,
it was time to walk away.

He started to go, but she caught his shoulders
in her small, gentle hands, somehow compelling
him to look down into her eyes one more time.
And then she rose on tiptoe, her lips moving
close to his.

So close he felt her breath.

He whispered, "What are you doing, Anna?"

"What my heart tells me, like you said," she
whispered back. And then she kissed him.

The power of it was beyond imagining. He
was as engulfed in the kiss—in the woman—as
a lifeboat would be by a hurricane. He felt her

heart, soft, and loving and pure. He smelled her scents, and heard her heartbeat inside his own chest. He tasted her kiss, and it was beyond anything he'd ever dreamed off. He wrapped his arms around her and held her to him, and they kissed and kissed and kissed.

And then, finally, he gave heed to the sense of self-preservation he'd built upon a foundation of pain and betrayal. He'd thought Cassandra's heart was pure, too. And he'd been wrong.

Sleep, he commanded. *Sleep, and remember me as but a pleasant dream. Sleep, Anna. And when you wake, follow your heart's desire, no matter what. I'll find you again before you die. And you will be offered a choice. I promise you that. But for now, sleep. Sleep, Anna. Sleep.*

Anna slept. He held her against him as her legs went weak, and he scooped her up into his arms and then sped through the night, carrying her at speeds far too fast for mortal eyes to observe him. He probed her mind to find where she lived, and he took her there. An attractive, one-story house with flower boxes in the windows. Yellow. It would sell easily.

He unlocked the doors with the power of his mind and laid her gently on her bed, and then he turned and forced himself to go away. It was, for some reason, far more difficult than it should have been.

An hour later he sank his teeth into the throat of a drunken pedophile in a stinking alley outside the bar the man had been visiting.

But as the rush of the blood hit him, carrying with it the pleasant burn of rum, his mind went back to the woman he'd kissed beneath the lighthouse. He saw her eyes, her face, her hair. He heard her voice, rough with tears. He tasted her mouth, felt her hands on him. He closed his eyes and for just a moment gave in to the fantasy that it was her blood he was drinking now. Her blood, rushing into his throat, warming his flesh, sizzling in his soul, filling him with power, with strength, with vigor and, God help him, with desire—for her.

A surge of ecstasy rose in him even as he released his victim. The man's body fell to the alley floor, and Diego tipped his head back and, in spite of himself, released a growling roar to the night. In that moment, pure primal power and unleashed lust washed through him, and he had no control.

As he brought his head level again, he heard voices, human ones.

"What the hell? Was that a freaking lion?"

"I never heard anything like that in my—"

"A bear? *Here?*"

"C'mon."

Crouching low, Diego pushed off with his powerful legs and shot upward, rocketlike, landing easily on the roof above even as the curious mortals arrived at the mouth of the alley and saw the dead man lying there.

He didn't stick around to see what happened next.

Chapter 3

Two months later...

Anna stood in what felt like the vastness of eternity. There was no clear boundary between the sea around her and the night sky above. The only visible difference was that the sky was dotted with glittering stars and the water was too choppy to reflect them back. On calm seas, she'd experienced nights when she honestly couldn't tell where the mirror of the sea ended and the sky began. Breathtaking. And peaceful.

She no longer feared dying. She imagined that the night sky above was a black canvas, and that behind it there was a light—that beautiful heavenly light talked about by near-death survivors. She imagined the stars as tears in the fabric, giving her tiny glimpses of that warm, loving glow. One more month, give or take, if Mary's predictions were true. And then she would be able to find out for herself.

Below, and all around, her there was water. Blue-black, with whitecaps appearing and vanishing again as if at random. But there was an order to it, she thought. One she couldn't see but felt on some level. There was order to everything. It all happened for a reason.

Beneath her feet, her boat, the *Spanish Angel,* rocked and bobbed at the whim of those waves. She'd furled her sails, dropped anchor for the night. There was a vague and brief rocky shoreline in sight, but only barely, off the starboard side. It was small enough that she suspected it was an island, but she had no desire to visit it. People, tourists, were not what she had come out here to experience.

She stood on the port side, near the bow, staring out at the endless expanse of sea and sky, and letting her focus go soft until the two blended into one. One living, breathing, heaving, moving entity. The great Whole. And she was a part of it. Alive or dead, a part of it she would remain.

Anna was at peace now. That night on the pier, in the hulking shadow of the lighthouse, she'd met an angel. Her own guardian angel, she thought. And the fact that he had the face of her dream lover, who'd hovered just beyond the edge of her dreams since she'd been a teenager, made him even more real.

Yes, she had probably imagined him. Maybe. Her subconscious had conjured just the image she had needed. He had broken through her grief and her worry and her pain, and given her permission to be selfish. To be happy, even, during the waning months of her life.

He'd seemed so real. She'd even given him a name, in her imagination. Diego. It had come to her during that imaginary kiss. She knew his voice, his touch, his kiss. God, his kiss. And that sense of him looking so deeply inside her that he knew her deepest thoughts, fears, longings.

She'd spent a great many hours pondering her angel while she'd been living blissfully at sea. There had been something otherworldly about him, and a faint trace of an accent—Spanish, in his case—the way there always seemed to be when people claimed to be channeling the words of a spirit guide. Or of an angel. He'd had that accent in her dreams, too, she recalled.

Hazy, those dreams. Vague. No real story to them, just images of him, of his eyes blazing into hers, his hand reaching out to touch her cheek. And a feeling of absolute love welling up inside her heart.

She'd thought, in her youth, that those had been glimpses of her soul mate. Her future partner, husband, lover. But now she knew better. She'd been glimpsing her own personal guardian angel. He had come to her that night and told her what she needed to hear. And when she passed from this life into the next, he would be there, waiting. She was actually looking forward to seeing him again.

She'd sold her home and her possessions, and she'd closed out all her bank accounts and cashed in her retirement. She'd quit her job. And then she had bought one thing for herself. Something she had always wanted.

She'd given part of the remaining money to her sister's kids, and she'd invited them to lunch at a fast-food joint where she used to take them when they were little, so she could deliver the money personally and have a chance to say goodbye. She told them that she was leaving the country

and didn't know when she would return. They'd
accused her of abandonment until they'd seen
the numbers on the cashier's checks she handed
them. Then their whining had gone silent and
the questions had begun.

But by then she'd already been on her way out
the door.

The rest of the money had gone for supplies,
that she stowed on the gift she had bought for
herself. This sailboat. She'd named her boat the
Spanish Angel, after the otherworldly being
who'd come to her on that night when all had
seemed lost.

And now she was doing what she had always
dreamed of doing. She was sailing down the East
Coast, embracing the ocean she had loved since
birth. She was riding the waves, and soaking
up the sun, and relishing the wind. She was
communing with dolphins, and whales, and
sharks, and seals, with seagulls and osprey and
birds and fish she had yet to identify. She was
meditating, and pondering the meaning of life
and the universe and spirituality. She was living.
For the first time in her life, now that she was
dying, she was truly *living.*

She'd saved enough money to keep herself
in food and fresh water and other essentials for

the three months Mary told her she might have left, with a little extra left over in case she lived longer. Honestly, though, she didn't think that was going to happen. She was sleeping more and more. And soon, she thought, it might not be safe to remain at sea, with no one at the helm in case she never woke up.

Then again, what did she have to lose, really?

As she stood there with the wind in her hair, she smiled and felt content right to her soul. She was happy, she realized. She didn't have a worry in the world. She had no bills to pay, no jobs to rush to, no phones to answer, no computer to crash, no email to answer, no people depending on her and expecting things of her. All she had to do was sail, and live, and breathe. Eat and sleep. Read and sing. Pray and meditate. Ride the waves, and dream of crossing to the other side, into her guardian angel's open arms. She wondered if it was sinful to feel the way she felt for him. Because her love for him, while pure and powerful, didn't feel at all platonic. But she supposed if there was anything wrong with that, he wouldn't have kissed her the way he had.

If she died tonight, she thought, she would die happy. And she would be even happier when she emerged on the other side. She could feel the antigen tugging her to sleep yet again. She'd managed to stay awake for six straight hours today. That was pretty good, for her.

She went below, to the little cabin, and fell asleep in a state of bliss.

She'd been sleeping pretty hard, as she tended to do these days, when she realized the wind was howling and water was rolling over her face. It was too dark to see, and she was completely disoriented; nothing in the room was where it belonged, and she couldn't tell which way was up or which way was down. And yet, she felt no panic. The water was warm. And if she drowned, so be it. Suddenly there was a crash, and her beautiful boat seemed to explode in a thousand directions, flying away from her like the expanding universe itself and leaving her in the open water, which was roiling, throwing her up and sucking her back down again. Lightning flashed over and over, and she gasped for air, blinking through saltwater to see brief strobing images. Jutting rocks. Broken boards. Foaming froth. Pouring rain. Heaving waters.

The instinctive urge to survive overwhelmed her even as her practical mind told her to just relax into the embrace of the sea. She was dying, anyway. What did it matter? But at that moment, in that instant, all she wanted was to keep her head above water, to keep sucking air into her lungs, and to struggle ever nearer to the rocks that had demolished her boat.

In desperation, she cried out, spewing water with her words. "Help me! Help me, someone!"

Diego was safely inside his cottage, the window shades up and shutters thrown wide, so that he could watch the rain, enjoy the electric light show that nature was putting on tonight. He loved storms. The pure, raw power of them. Right now, the wind was blowing the palms so that their fronds were nearly upright, and the vibration of the airwaves whisking around their variegated trunks made a hum that was not unlike the primal tone of a didgeridoo. The wind, that hum, the thunder, the crashing waves—together they created a symphony, and he listened in pure raw pleasure.

And then, a heartbeat later, his entire body quivered in awareness. Danger. Fear. Panic. What the hell was—

Help me! Help me, someone!

He felt the summons more than heard it, but

then realized he'd heard it, as well, just barely. Not only that, but he knew its source, knew it immediately, as her energy rushed into his awareness, filling him. The woman he'd seen two months before, near the lighthouse, the one who'd been weeping. The woman he'd kissed.

One of the Chosen, and one with whom he'd felt an instant and powerful bond.

That made her very dangerous to him.

And yet, he was unable to deny the gut-level drive to help her. He had no choice. Nor would he have done otherwise even if he could have. He pulled on a slicker, a black one, caped. He pulled a cap down over his ears. It would only be soaked through in a few minutes, but he wore it, anyway, then dashed out of his haven and into the heart of the storm.

He could move faster than any living thing. Fast enough so that he would not be detectable to human eyes, nor, he suspected, to most of the wildlife here—though he wasn't entirely sure about that. Still, he pushed himself to preternatural speeds through the storm, until he stood on the windward shore, and there he paused, listening—not just with his ears but with all his senses—and staring intently out at the violent sea.

"Where are you?" he asked aloud, but he sent the words out to her, too, using the power of his mind, knowing that might be the only way she, a mere mortal, would be able to hear him.

Rocks. Water. Can't...see....

He felt a wave smash into her face, felt it as if it were happening to him. It silenced her mind and pushed her downward, and he felt her consciousness fading.

No time for the boat. He shed the slicker and hat, and ran into the water, sensing her near the treacherous rocks that rose from the sea a few hundred yards from shore. He dove, arrowing through the waves toward her. Angling deeper, to escape the surface effect of the storm—which would have slowed him, though only slightly—he sped onward, his senses attuned to the essence of her. Flawlessly they guided him, and in only seconds he was wrapping his arms around her body and shooting upward.

They broke the surface, and he held her so her back was against his chest, one hand pulling her forehead back and up. "Breathe!" he commanded, with his mind and will as well as his voice.

She gulped in air and gasped, gurgled and choked. Water spewed from her lips.

"Again," he told her. "Breathe."

And again she inhaled. Her eyes were closed tight, her body still. No fight left in her. He turned them toward shore, struggling now. He couldn't just speed through the waves without forcing more water into her lungs. And it was difficult to make headway while keeping her head from submerging once more.

Lifting his own head, he called out, no longer speaking like a man. His voice was a high-pitched chitter instead. And within moments a dorsal fin appeared, pale amid the black water.

"Thank you, my friend," Diego said softly, gripping the slick fin with one hand, holding on to his charge with the other. The dolphin swam rapidly toward shore, chirping happily, the ever-cheerful demeanor unaffected by the storm.

Diego couldn't say the same for his own— although his darkening mood wasn't due to the storm itself, but to what it had carried to his beach. His haven.

A woman. One of the Chosen. And not just any one, but *this one*. This woman he'd met during what he'd taken as a chance encounter two months ago. He'd gone into seclusion forty-five years ago because of a woman just like her. He'd taken refuge far from the reach of human or vampire. And yet, she had come.

Hell, was history doomed to repeat itself—
even here?

"Far enough, Layla," he said, releasing the
dolphin and giving the animal a pat on the side
even as it turned and swam away. His feet sank
into the sandy sea-bottom, and he shifted the
woman around to face him, carrying her as
he strode up out of the waves, onto the beach
and then along the winding and well-worn path
through the forest to his cottage. His sanctuary.
A place where only one other being had ever
set foot, at least within his five-century-plus
lifespan.

Allowing someone else to visit the island had
proven disastrous. He had sworn that no one ever
would breech his sanctuary again. And yet, here
she was. And there was not one thing he could
do about it.

Chapter 4

Anna struggled to open her eyes, but they seemed to resist her efforts. It was no surprise. She had a lot more trouble waking up, and a lot more trouble *staying* awake, lately. She seemed to be becoming almost nocturnal. The sun's energy was just too much for her slowly weakening body, she supposed. Hadn't Mary told her that would happen? The essence of nighttime was so much softer, easier to take. Even on the boat, she'd...

The boat...

Her sailboat!

Her eyes flew open wide, and she sucked in a breath so sharply that it hurt her chest. Her arms flew out, hitting something that clattered to the floor, and she pushed herself upward all at once. And then, slowly, her wide-open eyes showed her that she was not in the ocean, fighting to keep her head above water, being battered by the waves and the storm. No. She was warm, and she was dry. The surface beneath her was soft, and the room around her, one of utter beauty and… peace.

Odd, that she would think that, but that was what it felt like to her. Peace.

The walls were red-brown wood, full of swirls and knots. There was a small cobblestone fireplace on one of them, with a rounded opening, and a glass screen in front. There were flames dancing and heat flowing. Huge windows lined the room, but they were all closed off now, by dark shutters from the outside. There were a few pieces of furniture, all apparently made of raw wood-slabs and coated in thick gleaming layers of shellac. Someone had attached legs to them to create tables, backs to create chairs, added cushions to some for relaxation. The one she rested on was a sort of fainting couch, she thought. She was lying on a brown plush pad, and matching pillows were tucked between her body and the wooden back, which was, she thought as she tugged one of the pillows aside, gorgeous. Hand carved to resemble the graceful body and long swooping neck of a swan.

Sitting up slowly, she looked down to see that her hands were clutching a cream-colored blanket made of the same sort of fabric one would use to make a baby's first teddy bear. So soft. And then she noticed the shirt she wore—it wasn't her own. It was a man's tank-style undershirt. White, ribbed. Her arms were bare. She lifted the blanket and saw she had on a pair of men's boxer shorts.

She tried to remember how she'd come to be here, who had rescued her from the storm-tossed sea that had devoured her beautiful sailboat. Her *Spanish Angel?* But for the life of her, she couldn't recall anything more than waking in the water, struggling to keep her head above the surface, choking on the brine, and finally losing her battle. Peace had surrounded her as she had gone sinking down. And peace was what she had awakened to just now.

Was this heaven? Did they dress you in men's underclothes in heaven? Did they heat heaven with a crackling wood-fire?

Maybe. If heaven was, as she had come to suspect through all her hours of pondering and meditation, what one expected it to be, then maybe this was her heaven. A private, cozy cottage, where she was warm and safe and dry. She'd always wanted a cabin of wood, with a cobblestone fireplace. If this were *really* heaven, her cottage would be situated on a beach.

Beside her luxurious bed were a pitcher of water and a wooden bowl filled with tropical fruit. There were figs and nectarines and berries. She didn't particularly like figs. Would there be figs if this were heaven?

She stared at the bowl and imagined a juicy steak appearing there. Just to test it out. But nothing happened. Where *was* she?

As her senses expanded, seeking more information, she heard no sounds of traffic outside, no horns or motors or sirens. She didn't even hear an occasional passing car.

She eased the blanket off and sat up straighter, then swung her legs around and lowered her bare feet to the floor. She started to stand, but a wave of dizziness put her right back down. Her head swam, and her body began to complain at her for daring to move at all. Pain pulsed, soft, then more loudly, from her back, from her legs, from her shoulders and one hip. The dizziness became an insistent throb, and she lowered her head into her hands, closing her eyes and moaning softly.

Not heaven, she thought. *Not even close. I'm definitely still in my body.*

"You shouldn't be trying to get up yet."

It was a voice. A familiar voice. Deep and resonant and male, with the accent she'd heard so many nights in her sleep. Her angel?

His hands closed on her shoulders, and he spoke again with concern. "Are you all right?"

She lifted her head slowly, expecting…she didn't know what. A radiant being in white robes with a halo floating above his head?

It wasn't quite that. But he *was* radiant. And so blessedly, blissfully familiar. His skin was light, for a man who was clearly of Latin descent. Oh, the usual coppery tones were there, but it was almost as if it were backlit somehow. And his beloved eyes… Deep brown eyes like chocolate left too long in the summer sun, and lashes so thick she was almost jealous. Her own only looked that way with the help of mascara and eyeliner. He came by them naturally, just like the heavy brows and the full lips.

"It's you," she whispered, and she almost choked on the tears that welled up in her throat. "I really am dead, then. Why does it still hurt?"

His eyes seemed to well up, or maybe she was just thinking that because her own were wet. "No, pretty one. You are not dead."

Was his voice as beautiful as it seemed? Or was she experiencing some sort of ecstatic state induced by nearly drowning? "If I'm not dead, then…how can you be here with me?" she asked softly.

He frowned, then lifted a hand to indicate the room around them. "This is my home. Where else would I be?"

"Then…you're not an angel?"

His smile was quick, but restrained, too. A flash of perfect white teeth only partly revealed. "No, *pequita,* I am no angel."

"But I know you. I do. I know you. We've met before. At the lighthouse, before I…" Her head ached harder, and she frowned, pressing her hand to her forehead.

"You've been through a terrible trauma. Your mind is playing tricks on you, no doubt."

"No, I *do* know you. I've dreamed of you. All my life, really. When you came to me that night—"

"Your mind is playing tricks on you."

"No. You knew my name that night. You called me Anna. And I know yours. It's Diego."

That seemed to bring him up short. He went still, and his gaze darted away from hers, turning inward, but only very briefly. "I've been speaking to you while you slept, Anna. I've told you my name several times. But this is the first time I've heard yours."

"Why are you lying to me?" she asked softly.

He met her eyes again, holding her gaze steadily as if to show her how sincere he was being. How truthful. "You've been through a terrible ordeal. That's just confusing you now. And it doesn't matter, anyway, does it? The past rarely does, you know. You are here with me now, safe and sound, and I can get you back to your people just as quickly as you wish. So there's not a thing in the world for you to worry about."

She nodded very gently, even while thinking that she had no "people" to go back to, and now no boat and no money.

"You should lie back down. Your poor body is bruised and battered from end to end. You need rest, so you can heal."

She thought so, too, but didn't obey. Not yet. "How badly am I hurt?"

"Nothing is broken, *pequita,* and I don't detect

any internal injuries. I think it would be harder on you to make the journey to the mainland in your current state than it would be to just remain for a few days and let your body heal."

"The mainland?" She frowned and lifted her head again. "Where are we?"

"We're on my island. I call her Serenity, because that is what she has given me."

"Your island?"

"Yes."

"And…you live here with…?"

"With the animals. With the birds. With the ocean waves and the palms and the coconuts. And…with peace."

"There's no one else?"

"No. No one else." He shrugged. "Until now. But I promise you, you are safe with me. I will not harm you. And I'll take you back as soon as—"

"Can I see it? I need to see it—please."

"The island?"

"Yes. Please, Diego, I need to see it."

He hesitated, staring at her as if trying to see more than what she was saying, and she experienced the oddest sensation, as if he were probing her very soul. And then he seemed to make a decision. He bent closer, sliding his arms underneath her body and lifting her up.

"Wait! You don't have to carry me."

"You're in no condition to walk on your own. And it's not the first time, after all." She barely had time to glimpse the other rooms in his home as he swept through them toward a large wooden door that seemed to be made from one single board and was completely covered with the images of animals and symbols, like she would have expected to see on some Native totem pole.

He nodded at the handle, which was a wrought-iron ring. "If you would," he said.

She grasped it and pulled. And the door swung open, revealing…paradise. Stone paths wound in a dozen directions amid exotic flowering plants, the likes of which she had never seen. Orchids, maybe. Birds-of-paradise, perhaps. And others, huge blossoms and tall grasses, all emitting the most beautiful fragrances she'd ever smelled. There was a fire circle in the center of it all, made of stacked rocks, with a bare, sandy patch of ground surrounding it and a chair entirely carved from a tree trunk close beside. Beyond the flowers and paths and fire circle, palm trees stood tall and graceful, along with other trees she couldn't have named. And beyond those she saw a very large roof. "What's that?"

"My workshop. I'm building a new sail-boat."

A tiny animal—like a miniature deer—grazed nearby. Its head came up, soft eyes meeting hers, nostrils flaring slightly. But it didn't run away. It looked at the man who held her, and he looked back. Anna watched his face, more caught up in his expression than the odd little animal. He looked at it the way an adoring father looks at his child. He loved it. He smiled at it, and she looked back at the tiny deer as it returned to grazing. Something moved in her peripheral vision, and she glimpsed a peacock strutting along one of the winding paths that led into the forest, its long tail dragging behind.

She looked and looked and looked. And the more she looked, the more beauty she saw unfolding beneath the nighttime sky, that was clear and glittering with stars. And then, slowly, she swung her wide eyes to his again and asked, "Are you *sure* this isn't heaven?"

Chapter 5

Diego was both pleased and troubled by her reaction to the haven he'd created. Pleased, because it gave him pride to share what he had chosen to surround himself with. The natural beauty. The place he'd worked on until it became his idea of paradise. And yes, heaven, because he would never see the real thing, being an immortal. Or if he did, he wasn't sure he would be allowed in. Weren't vampires damned?

The only thing his paradise lacked was the presence of other people. But he'd chosen to make it that way. And he'd protected his solitude with every power at his disposal.

But he was worried by her reaction, too, because she seemed to love Serenity Island just a little bit too much. He didn't want her here any longer than she had to be. And that was a difficult thought to maintain while holding her cradled in his arms, her body resting against him, her arms linked around his neck.

She twisted to look over his shoulder, back at the house, a two-story structure of logs and cobblestones. "It's like something out of a fairy tale," she said. "Did you build it?"

He nodded, realized her striking sea-blue gaze was no longer focused on him and spoke. "Yes. Over the course of…several years."

"But how?" she asked, her wide eyes meeting his once more. "There were lights inside…I saw—"

"I use the sun and the wind." He pointed with his chin, since his arms were busy holding her. Her eyes followed his gaze to the windmill standing on the highest hill on the island, visible like a sentinel in the distance. He'd had to anchor it in place the night of the storm, but he'd since set it free again. Then he showed her the solar panels lined up on the roof of his home. There were more at the workshop. "Batteries store the excess. I'm never short of power here."

She drew her eyes from the roof to gaze into his once more. "The world could learn a lot from a man like you."

"I want no part of the world," he whispered.

She swallowed, silent for a moment, searching, and he felt almost as if she were probing his mind the way he had probed hers. But she wasn't capable of such a trick, was she? She was no vampire. And yet he felt himself erecting a mental barrier to his mind, the way he would do were some strange vampire trying to read thoughts he wanted to keep to himself.

"Where did you get the lumber?" she asked at length. "The stone?"

"From the mainland," he explained. "A little at a time. All *Maria* could carry in a single trip, and then back for more when I ran out."

"Maria?" she asked, tilting her head to one side.

The wind lifted her hair and made it dance. He nearly lost himself in watching it.

"My sailboat. The *Santa Maria XIII*."

She frowned very slightly. "That name inspires about a half dozen questions."

He looked away. "It's just a name."

"Somehow I doubt that." She waited, but when

he didn't elaborate, she went on. "And you live here all alone?"

"It's the way I prefer it." Had he sounded a little defensive just then? He wondered.

"I've been doing something very similar myself. Bought a sailboat and set out, all alone. There's something about being one-on-one with the sea and the sky that just—"

"Nourishes the soul," he said softly.

"Yes. And clears the mind. It feels…holy. Like a sacred pilgrimage, somehow. Is that how it is for you, too?"

"I…love this island. And I love the natural beings that inhabit it. Every plant and animal and bird. I'm not quite as fond of people."

She nodded as if she understood that sentiment, but she didn't elaborate. After a few moments she said, "The sky is so clear now. It's hard to believe it was so violent only hours ago."

He carried her to the log chair and lowered her into it, since holding her was so very disturbing. He'd fed, and fed well, hoping to alleviate the natural cravings that he knew would arise in him with her close by. Oh, he couldn't harm her. But drinking from her didn't have to harm her. Quite the opposite, in fact. And warm, living blood was so much more enticing than the cold, bagged liquid that usually lined the refrigerator in his tiny kitchen. He'd created it in case of interlopers, to make it look as if an ordinary mortal lived there. No food in the cupboards, but there were dishes.

Since her arrival, he'd moved all the bagged blood to the cooler in the workshop, so she wouldn't stumble upon it by accident. He didn't need her knowing what he was—not yet. He wasn't ready. And she still had time.

Even as he lowered her into the chair, he sensed the warm, living blood pulsing just beneath her delicate skin. Enticing him. He couldn't remember the last time he'd—

Yes, he could. And it was far better if he didn't.

"It's been almost twenty-four hours, actually, since your ship was dashed against the barrier rocks offshore," he told her.

She shot him a quick look, her brows arching. "I slept the entire day?"

He nodded. "Don't sound so appalled. I did, as well."

"Well, no wonder, after the night you must have had." He lowered his eyes. "And I'm not appalled that I did. I do most of the time. More and more, in fact. But I want to know more,

Diego. How did it happen?" she asked. "How did you know I was in trouble?"

He pursed his lips and averted his eyes, knowing that the truth would sound unbelievable. She would either guess that he wasn't quite human or presume he was lying to make himself sound like a superman. And he didn't like either option. So he chose a third. He lied.

"I was out for a late-night stroll and found you lying on my beach, in the surf."

"Must have been a shock to you."

He shrugged.

"So you picked me up and carried me back to your...your home."

"What else could I do? Certainly not leave you there to die."

"And you undressed me," she whispered, her voice going deeper, softer.

"It had to be done. Your clothes were soaked." He paced away a few steps, then added, "But they're clean and dry now."

"I owe you more than I can ever hope to repay," she said softly. "And I'm sorry to have interfered with your solitude."

"It's not as if you had a choice in the matter."

"Still...I'll try not to bother you overly much."

She shrugged. "In fact, you'll probably rarely see me. I've become almost entirely nocturnal. There's something about the sun that makes me sleepy. The night, though…that brings me alive. At least as much as anything can, these days."

He frowned at her, even while wondering if that was a side effect of having the Belladonna antigen. He didn't remember it bothering him when he'd been human, but then again, he'd been young when he'd been given the Dark Gift. Twenty-five. She had to be in her mid-thirties, at least. Perhaps even a bit older. Few of the Chosen lived to see forty. They either became what he was—a vampire—or they quietly died. Mostly the latter, since few ever knew the truth about what the antigen in their blood meant, much less knew a vampire they could ask to transform them.

He realized how little he knew about her and what she was experiencing. He wanted to know more, but not now. She looked tired. Weak.

"You're pale," he said. "We should get you back inside."

"But it's so beautiful out here. Can't we stay a little longer?"

He tilted his head to one side in thought, then nodded his consent and moved to the fireplace.

He'd built it by digging a bowl out of the sandy soil, then lining it with stones so tightly interlocked that it was as if they'd been laid with cement. The surface surrounding it was lined with angle-cut stones in an ever-widening circle. He'd cleared the area around that, as well, so that no spark would ever land and set fire to his haven. Usually he used a domed screen to cover it, for even greater protection.

As a vampire, he had more than one reason to fear open flames. And yet there was something so primal and so pleasing about them that he couldn't resist. His kind had a love-hate relationship and an abiding fascination with fire. Maybe that came from never being able to see the sun.

As always, the kindling stood nearby, and he bent to work, building a small campfire for her. As he worked, she spoke.

"You don't have to stay out here just because I am. If you want to go to bed, I mean…"

"I tend to be a bit nocturnal myself," he told her.

"Really?" She frowned, and he knew she found that odd and wanted to ask why, wanted to dig a little. But she restrained herself with a sigh and moved on to a new subject. "Can you see the ocean from here? I haven't caught a glimpse of it yet."

"From the second story you can. But there's only my bedroom up there. And the bathroom, of course." With a luxurious tub and shower he adored, and a toilet that had been installed just in case his hideaway was ever discovered. It was a cover. But it was a working toilet. It hadn't been used since the last time a mortal had set foot on this island. Cassandra. But he wasn't going to think about her.

"What made you build so far from the shore?" she was asking.

"Shelter from the storms. Privacy from any passing ships that might grow curious. But it's only a short walk along that path to the beach. And you can hear the ocean from here. Listen."

She did. He watched her close her eyes to listen, saw the way her senses sharpened, and knew the moment she heard the waves whispering over the beach by the way her entire being practically sighed in contentment. Yes, this place had that same effect on him.

And then her eyes opened again. "I know the full name of your sailboat, but not yours," she said. "Who is the man who saved my life?"

He rose from where he'd been hunkered by the fire, put a palm flat against his waist and bowed slightly toward her. "Diego del Torres," he said.

Smiling, she said, "I'm Anna Seville."

But he already knew that. He'd known it from the night he'd met her, two months ago. It was a name that had been whispering through his mind ever since. "I'm very glad you didn't die, Anna Seville."

Her eyes lowered quickly, as if to hide some rush of emotion, and he heard her mind's knee-jerk response. *I'm dying soon, anyway. I thought I was ready, but now that I've met you, seen this place... I'm not sure of anything anymore.*

But aloud she only said, "I'm glad, too. Otherwise, I wouldn't have had the chance to see this beautiful place, and to meet you. Thank you for saving my life, Diego."

"You are more than welcome." He stared into her eyes—and into her mind—for a long moment, then finally decided to say what needed to be said. "And that is true, Anna, despite what I'm going to say next. And I hope you won't take offense."

"You saved my life. I think you've earned the right to say whatever you feel you have to."

He nodded. "You cannot stay here."

She frowned, all the pleasure vanishing from her face.

"A day or two more, yes, naturally, while you recover from your injuries, but once you're well enough to travel, I will have to take you back to the mainland."

Her eyes shifted away from his, and she blinked rapidly. "I understand. This is your haven. Mine was broken to bits by the storm. That doesn't give me the right to horn in on yours."

He nodded slowly. "I'm glad you understand." He wanted to say more, but there was a feeling creeping over him, one he knew all too well. "It's nearly sunrise."

She seemed to shake off the discomfort—hurt, perhaps—his words had inspired in her and looked at him again. "I want to watch it come up over the ocean. Can we?"

"Sadly, no. I have…I have a severe sensitivity to sunlight, Anna. That's the condition that has forced me to become…nocturnal, as you put it earlier. And I need to retire soon."

She blinked, opened her mouth, then closed it again. "I suppose you've heard all the vampire jokes you care to by now."

He felt his eyes widen a little but schooled his expression at once. "More than I care to, in fact."

"Don't let me keep you, then," she said softly.

He nodded. "I don't think you're in any condition to walk to the beach to watch that sunrise. Not today, at least. Perhaps tomorrow morning?"

She nodded. "You're probably right. If I find myself too weak to walk back, I most likely won't be able to rouse you. If you sleep soundly, that is." She tilted her head. "Do you? Sleep soundly, I mean?"

"Like the dead." He said it with a straight face, saw her expressionless reaction last for an expanded moment, and then she smiled.

"I get it. Vampire joke."

He returned the smile with a wink. "Make yourself comfortable here, Anna. While you were asleep, I stocked the house with fruit and spring water. There are fresh fish in the kitchen if you need more sustenance than that. I caught them for you earlier. Enjoy the day. I'll see you this evening."

She frowned at him, but nodded. "All right.

Good night, then." She rolled her eyes. "Good day, I mean. I guess."

"Just say 'good rest.'"

"Okay, that, then."

"Do you want me to help you back inside before I go?"

She seemed to think about it, this involved thrusting her lower lip out just a little, a habit he was already finding he enjoyed. "No," she said at length. "I'll stay outside a bit longer. I think I can manage to limp back into the house when I'm ready."

"Be careful. Take your time."

"I will."

He nodded, sensing that she would not listen to him, anyway, and walked away, wondering if his secrets were safe. He'd taken every precaution he could think of to ensure they would be.

He'd done much the same when Cassandra had shown up here, only to learn later that her innocence had been an act, and that she had known what he was from the very start and set out on a mission to seduce him, to use him, to get what she wanted from him and then walk away forever.

And that was precisely what she had done.

It was not going to happen to him again.
Not ever.

Not even with Anna Seville.

Chapter 6

Anna wasn't afraid of him. That might seem very odd to anyone else, she supposed. Maybe it ought to seem odd to her. Or foolish, even. Here she was, alone, on an apparently deserted tropical island, with the strangest man she had ever met. What did he mean, he'd stocked the house with fruit and water and fresh fish *for her?* What did *he* eat?

He might be strange, but he was also beautiful. She had rarely chosen that word to describe a man, but she could think of no more suitable one. The liquid brown of his eyes and those impossibly thick lashes. The slenderness of his face and the angular jawline. Skin so smooth it seemed unreal.

All alone, yes, but perhaps not lonely. A genius, of sorts. He must be, to have built what he had here. The fairy-tale house, the natural sources of power, the entire layout, that was so very Zen-like with its beautiful landscaping. He'd created a paradise for himself. And no one else.

He was a solitary, ingenious artist who lived his life by night. And whose voice and face were familiar to her. Even his name, Diego, was exactly what she had known it would be. In fact, the only thing about him that seemed strange to her was that he was human and not the guardian angel she'd been expecting.

Maybe she really *was* dead. Maybe this was heaven.

She looked down at her legs, stretched out in front of her as she relaxed in the low tree-trunk chair, that was surprisingly comfortable. The firelight gave her a better look at herself than she'd had before, and what she saw made her suck in a sharp breath that caused a stabbing pain in her sore chest.

Her legs were mottled in vivid bruises that spanned the color spectrum from brilliant fuchsia to deep gray. They looked like contour maps of mountain ranges. There were scrapes, too, but mostly deep bruises. No wonder it hurt to walk. Lifting the waistband of the boxer shorts, she saw that the bruising included her hips and, as she twisted in her seat, her buttocks, as well. She looked as if she'd been beaten with a club.

She held out her arms and saw that they, too, were badly bruised, then shuddered at the thought of what her face must look like. She needed to go find a mirror. He'd said there was a bathroom upstairs, hadn't he?

She would definitely pay it a visit before too much longer. But first, she was dying to get a look around the island, and his warnings about her being too weak to walk to the beach had fallen on deaf ears. She'd been alone at sea for eight weeks now. She thought she could handle a walk, even with bruises for company.

So she set out, and it did hurt. Every step brought pain, and she supposed that was all the proof she needed that she wasn't dead and this wasn't the afterlife. Yet it did not erase from her mind the knowledge that there was something otherworldly going on here. Something about him, or this island.

Or both.

It really did hurt to walk. Maybe he'd been right, she thought, once she'd traipsed a few dozen yards into the palms. She did seem to be limping a bit more with every step. Still, she pressed on, walking very slowly along a well-worn footpath that twisted and writhed through the forest. And even as she traversed the trail, night began to give birth to the day. The sky paled slightly, and in the space of a heartbeat the hush around her was filled with bird calls as the forest came to raucous life.

She smiled at their songs, their cries, their screeches, and wished she could identify them by their voices. Maybe if she were here long enough she could make a study of them.

But, of course, she wouldn't be here long at all. Diego had made that much perfectly clear, hadn't he?

Such a beautiful place to live, she thought. And then another thought followed on its heels. Such a beautiful place to die.

She knew she should have felt at peace with that thought. Just as she had come to a peaceful acceptance of her own demise while she'd been at sea. Gradually she'd understood that this was just part of the journey. She'd accepted her own end, had started looking forward to seeing what was on the other side.

Of course, that had been when she'd still thought he would be waiting for her there. Her Spanish angel, Diego.

Now she no longer felt peaceful about it at all. In fact, thinking about her life ending filled her with an uncomfortable sense of foreboding. Of unease. Of near panic. What the hell had happened to her serenity?

She emerged from the tree line onto an expanse of white sand that sloped ever so gently to the sea. Waves rolled in, broke and thinned until they were little more than froth on the sand, and then the sea sucked them back again. Over and over. A hypnotic, healing energy wafted over her, as if generated by the movements of those waves.

Live in the moment, she reminded herself. Make the very most of every single moment. Just like you've been doing for the past two months. Just be in the moment, and don't think too much about the future.

Yes. That felt marginally better.

She sank down onto the sand, drawing her knees to her chest and gazing outward toward the horizon. And she saw the blazing hint of fire that touched the sky at the very end of the sea—for just an instant, until it became a glowing curve. Then the edge of the giant dinner-plate sun, rising as if from the depths of the ocean itself.

It was beautiful here, she thought, smiling. She really didn't think she was going to want to leave.

Diego had slept with his bedroom door locked, something he hadn't felt the need to do since he'd hosted the only other houseguest ever to visit Serenity Island. He didn't need another woman poking around, uncovering his secrets. Perhaps exposing them this time, and his haven with them. There was too much at stake. And he knew, from cruel experience, that once she had what she wanted her apparent enchantment with his home and his island—not to mention with him—would evaporate. Because it wasn't real. He gathered up fresh clothing and took it with him into the bathroom, where he indulged in his nightly ritual of a piping hot shower. It felt delicious against his supersensitive skin. Vampires felt *everything* more powerfully than humans did. Pleasure. Pain, too.

If anything, he thought as he stood beneath the steaming spray, Anna was even more beautiful than Cassandra had been. Her essence, her aura, was like a soft golden glow. The impression she gave was of a pure spirit, good to her core. But tender, too. Vulnerable. Easily frightened. Of course, that could just be what she wanted him to believe. She might be very good at disguising her true motives. Blocking her thoughts. It wasn't impossible. Some mortals could do it. Cassandra could.

Maybe Anna was...

She wasn't in the house.

He realized it as he basked in the shower's pulsing flow. There was no sense of his wounded houseguest whatsoever.

He cranked off the shower knobs, stopping the flow of the solar-heated water, and stood there dripping, cocking his head to one side, feeling for her. Then he frowned. Her essence was there, but distant. Near the beach, he thought.

Stepping out of the shower stall, he toweled off, dressed in khaki trousers and a short-sleeved yellow shirt, then headed down the stairs and outside. His hair was still wet, and he was barefoot. But then, he was nearly always barefoot. He walked, gathering his hair in a band behind his head. The shirt still hung unbuttoned, but it was a warm night, and he loved the air on his skin. Often he didn't wear any clothes at all. Why bother? He was entirely alone here, aside from the animals he so loved.

As he emerged onto the beach, he saw her curled on one side, sleeping in the sand. Close beside her Charlie, a familiar iguana, stood in the stand, poised and motionlessly staring at her face. As if waiting for her to wake up.

Certain she'd been there for a while, Diego knelt beside her, and put a hand on her shoulder. "Anna. Wake up, now."

She smiled in her sleep, twisting a little, rubbing her cheek over her shoulder. "Hmm?"

"Wake up now," he repeated, trying not to notice how irresistibly attracted he was to her in this state. Or any state, he corrected. "Come on."

Her beautiful eyes opened, like jewels shining on him with a power that surprised him. And then, as she noticed the animal so near her face, her smile become full blown. "Well, hello there, little guy." She met the reptile's steady gaze, and her own was nonthreatening. Almost beaming with love. Lifting a hand, she tentatively stroked one crooked finger over Charlie's neck.

The iguana leaned into her touch the way an

affectionate cat might do. So much for loyalty, Diego thought.

"I think he likes you," he said, and then he sighed. "Anna, meet Charlie. He's an Acklins iguana, and he's quite upset that he's not looking his best right now. Those browns and greens, though quite lovely, brighten up to oranges and yellows during the hottest parts of the day, or so I've read."

The lizard gave a slow, contented blink, then turning, skittered away into the undergrowth, his very gait a comedy of its own.

Anna laughed. "Do you name all the animals who live here?"

"Only the ones I get to know well," he said.

She was still smiling. It was hard to believe she might be up to no good, conniving or plotting to use him. Hard to believe there was anything other than sweetness in her, when she smiled at him like that.

"I can't believe I fell asleep." She pushed her hands through her auburn curls, that were more beautiful tousled than neat, he thought.

"How long have you been out here?"

She blinked, her gaze sliding from his to the sea, the horizon, the night sky. "All day," she said, sounding only slightly surprised. "I watched the sunrise."

"You're lucky you didn't burn to a crisp," he told her. Then he tipped his head up, noticing the thick fronds of the palm above her. "This tree must like you as much as Charlie did. She protected you."

"She?" Her eyes followed his, and she examined the graceful tree, the way its trunk bent over and its fronds draped low, giving her shade for almost the entire day. "It does look rather feminine at that."

"You must be starving."

"I am." She extended a hand. "Help me up?"

Diego clasped her hand and pulled her onto her feet with him; then, turning, he began walking her back along the footpath toward the house. "Aside from hunger, how do you feel?"

She shot him a quick look. "I'm very sore. Way more than I realized. I hurt all over." She slowed her pace, added a pronounced limp. "I thought I was strong enough to walk down to the beach and back, but...you were right. I think my body took a far worse beating out there on the rocks than I knew."

He sensed that she was being less than

perfectly honest and delved into her mind, just a little. He felt her pain, the stiffness, the aches. They were bad, yes. But she was pouring it on a bit more than she would normally do, and he heard, clearly, her rationale. *Don't act like you're doing too well, dummy, or he'll be hauling you back to the mainland before the night is out. Besides, you're not doing all that well.*

Just as he'd suspected. She was playing it up so she could stay here longer. And that certainly lent credence to his suspicion that she had come out here knowing already what he was and what he could do for her. She had come out here to trick him into sharing the Dark Gift with her.

When all she had to do was ask.

Or maybe…maybe he was wrong. Hell, how could he know for sure?

"Did you enjoy the sunrise, at least?" he asked, to keep her talking. Because the more he conversed with her, the more of herself she revealed. Soon he would see all her secrets.

She stopped walking to beam up at him. "It was most beautiful one I've ever seen, Diego." She met his eyes as she said it, then looked beyond him, shaking her head. "This entire place—it's like your own personal Eden."

"That's exactly how I think of it."

She smiled. "I'm very grateful to you for putting up with my presence for a little while. It's awfully generous of you to share this special place with a stranger. Although…" She stopped there, gnawing her lower lip in a way that made him want to taste it.

"Although?" he prompted.

Tipping her head up, she stared into his eyes. "You don't feel like a stranger to me at all."

Like a magnet, she pulled him nearer. Not physically, but with those eyes. They tugged, and he felt his head begin to lower, his eyelids begin to fall. But he caught himself, blinking free of the spell she'd cast and straightening up again.

She lowered her head quickly, almost as if embarrassed. "I don't suppose that makes any sense to you, does it?"

"It doesn't matter if it makes sense to me. And it's not as if this is the first time you've mentioned it. It's your feeling, and you have a right to it." He set off toward the house again, step by step, though she seemed to want to take it very slowly.

"It's just that…well, it goes back to the worst day of my life, or what I thought at the time was the worst. About two months ago." She looked over at him as they walked.

He wasn't touching her anymore, but it was all he could do not to. He wanted to slide an arm around her waist, to hold her against him. He wanted to help her, because he could feel the discomfort that walking brought, but also the pleasure she was taking in the stroll.

Touching her right then, he decided, would be a mistake. He met her eyes briefly, to let her know he was listening, even though he thought he knew what she was about to say.

"Actually, it goes back a lot further than that. I'd been seeing a face, hearing a voice, in my dreams since I was a teenager. I thought I was seeing my soul mate then. But later I decided he was someone else entirely."

"He?"

"You."

He lifted his brows, studying her.

"But back to that night, two months ago. I'd been feeling…tired. Lethargic. Sleeping more and more, and sometimes during the day, too." She smiled. "Like you."

He smiled back but didn't interrupt.

"It seemed to keep getting worse, so I finally saw a doctor. And she told me…" She paused, as if needing to gather her strength to go on. "She told me I was dying."

Then she looked at him again as if to gauge his reaction. But it didn't seem appropriate to feign shock or surprise. "I'm sorry, Anna. That must have been extremely difficult for you to hear."

"It was. I was…I was devastated, really. But then…then I wasn't."

He lifted his brows.

"I just had to process it all. My life was ending. And I think what I really regretted was that I'd never lived. I'd spent my life taking care of others—people who never even seemed all that appreciative of it. Mary—my doctor—she tried to tell me that, but I didn't really get it, you know? Not down deep. Not until I wandered down to the harbor, where all the sailboats come in. I've always loved the sea, always wanted to buy a sailboat and just head out into the ocean alone. No worries. No cares."

"And what's kept you from doing that up to now?" he asked, honestly curious.

She shrugged. "My sister. Well, her kids, really. She's an addict."

"Heroin?"

"Prescriptions. Anything she can get her hands on, really. Vicodin, Percocet, Ativan, Oxy." She shrugged. "I gave up trying to help her long ago. She has to want to help herself, and she just doesn't. But she has two kids, and they needed me. So I was there for them. I mean, they lived with her, but I was the one making sure there was always food in the house, keeping the power from being shut off and the heat on. I was the one who bought all their school clothes, and went to all the open houses and parent-teacher conferences and holiday concerts. I was the one who kept Child Protective Services from declaring her unfit and taking them away from her for good."

He nodded, and he knew she was underselling all she had done, minimizing it.

"The kids grew up and headed off to college. Now they both have jobs, they're living on their own—not high on the hog or anything. But they support themselves, and over time they'll do even better. So I stopped paying my sister's bills." She looked at him, as if waiting for his verdict on that. But he said nothing, and so she went on. "See, when I paid them before, it was for the kids' sake, but now it would just make me an enabler. She's not going to take care of herself unless she's forced to. It's the best thing I can do for her."

"You don't have to defend your actions to me, Anna. Not only am I not your judge, I agree with your decision completely. I doubt I'd have done as much as you have, in your position."

She thinned her lips. "I love my sister."

"That I *will* judge. You *don't* love your sister. You love who she could be, maybe who she once was and who she could become again. But you don't love who she is now. A negligent mother, an addict without the backbone to get herself clean. Who could love that? What is there to love in that?"

She lowered her head. He thought her eyes were growing moist. "When I refused to keep helping her, the kids disowned me. They won't even speak to me anymore."

"And how long did all of this happen before you were handed your…prognosis?" He'd been about to say "death sentence," then decided it was too harsh.

"A few months."

He nodded slowly.

"So, anyway, that's where I was in my life that night, as I sat on the pier by the lighthouse, staring out at the ocean and crying and wishing someone would step in and tell me what to do. And that's when I…had this…encounter."

He lifted his brows but didn't meet her eyes. "Encounter?"

"Vision, maybe? Maybe it all happened inside my head. But it was very clear, very vivid. Like it was real. I met…this man. The same man I'd been dreaming about all my life. He came to me, and he held me, and he told me it would be a sin not to live what was left of my life to the fullest, doing what I had always wanted to do most. He said that was our whole reason for being here in the first place."

"Sounds like a very wise man."

"It was you, Diego," she said softly. She stopped walking, staring up at him. Forcing him to meet her steady, probing gaze. "I swear, it was you. How is that possible?"

He had to hold her eyes, but it was very difficult for him to lie to her when she was looking at him so intently. In fact, he didn't think he could. But for the life of him, he couldn't sense deception in her just now. He didn't think she knew what he was, not in that moment.

"Is it possible," he asked, "that you were feeling so low that the man you believe you met that night seemed to…to save you? And that since I also saved you, though in a different way, your subconscious mind has created a connection that wasn't there before?"

She blinked, and a tiny crease appeared right

above the bridge of her nose. He had to restrain himself from bending to kiss it away. "I...hadn't thought of it that way."

"It's just a notion," he said. Then he paused, as a tawny-colored bat flew from a nearby palm, swooping and diving right over her head. She caught her breath, ducking at first, from sheer instinct, but then straightening and watching with awe.

"I've never seen a bat that color before."

"That's Buffy."

She grinned so wide he almost laughed. "After the vampire slayer?" she asked.

He was stunned by those words and stared at her, his eyes no doubt wide with horror. "Vampire...*slayer?*"

"The television show. It was...well, obviously you've never seen it."

He sighed, relief flooding him. "No. No television reception out here. Nor would I want there to be."

She nodded. "So then why name the bat 'Buffy'?"

"It's her name. She's a buffy flower bat. They supposedly only live in the Bahamas, but she's living proof otherwise."

She smiled, then lifted her eyes and her hand,

wiggling her fingers. "Hey, Buffy." She kept watching the bat's antics. "She looks so carefree. Not a worry in the world."

"What is there to worry about, after all?" he asked.

She tilted her head sideways, looking at him curiously. "Dying?"

"Humans are born dying," he told her. "It's as natural as the sun setting at night. Part of the cycle. It's all fine. Everything's fine." He watched her taking that in, and then, when she seemed to have absorbed it, he went on. "What did you do, after that night when the...the vision told you it was all right to live as you wanted to?"

She met his eyes. "I did what I wanted to." And then she smiled. "I put my house on the market, quit my job, wrote my will, planned my funeral—all the next day. And then I started looking for a sailboat. And you know, it was as if the day I learned I was dying, I finally started living."

"And you've been at sea ever since?" he asked.

"Until that storm, yes. I was hoping my boat would outlive me, but, um, it didn't work out that way. And now I'm not sure what I'm going to do. When I leave here, I mean."

He nodded, saying nothing. The conversation had taken a turn for the awkward.

"Because I have no home to return to, no job, no money, and only another month or so before I'm due to…you know…check out. If it all goes down the way Mary said it would."

"It *is* a dilemma," he agreed, and then he nodded. "Here we are. Why don't you cook some of that fish while I take care of a few chores around the island, hmm?"

She frowned at him, but nodded. "Chores?"

"I'd like to spend some time working on my new sailboat. In the workshop."

She smiled. "I'd love to see it sometime." Then she frowned. "But I'm so tired just from the walk back from the beach, I don't think—"

"There will be another time. You'll love this boat, being a sailor yourself. She's all wood, twice as big as the *Santa Maria XIII*."

She smiled, visualizing. "How close are you to being ready for her maiden voyage?"

He shrugged. "A few more weeks. No longer." He smiled at her eager excitement over his project, a work of the heart, truly. And he found himself eagerly anticipating taking her out to his workshop, showing her the boat, watching her reactions. Damn, she was getting to him. Far too deeply.

She was staring back at him, deep into his eyes, and looking as if she wanted to do more… as if she wanted to embrace him. But she held herself off and said, "Go ahead, then. I'll make enough fish for both of us, if you want."

"No need. I've…already eaten." He hadn't, and that was part of the problem, wasn't it? He was hearing the gentle call of her, the thrumming rush of blood flowing through her veins just beneath her supple, warm, salty skin, and it was doing things to his mind. Making him want to blurt that she should just stay here, with him, for the time she had left. Making him want to take her in his arms, to taste her skin, just a little. Maybe take a sip, one tiny droplet, to sate himself.

Right. And then the next thing he knew, he would begin to care for her. To believe that she cared for him, too. And then he would tell her that she didn't have to die. That she could live by night, endless night, as he did. He would tell her what he was, and offer to share the Dark Gift with her.

And she would pretend shock and surprise, and then calm, beautiful acceptance, and she would accept the Gift. He would drink from her, drain her to the very edge of oblivion, and then he would feed her from his own veins. And she would awaken a newborn vampire, a fledgling with wonder in her eyes.

And then she would leave him, laughing at his naive belief that there would be some fairy-tale ending, some happily ever after, for the two of them. She would leave him, laughing at his innocence, his trust. She would leave him, alone, in the paradise he had wanted to share.

He saw it all playing out in his mind, the memory stabbing into his heart like a red-hot blade. Cassandra laughing at how easily he had fallen for her. Laughing as she told him she had what she had come for and would be leaving now. Calling him a sap—and worse.

No, he would not fall so easily again. Not again.

Chapter 7

He left her at the door, and as Anna watched him go, she felt a sense of clarity. That was, she supposed, the positive side of facing one's imminent demise. Clarity. It suddenly became very, *very* easy to see what was important and what was not. It became easy to know what you wanted and almost impossibly irrational to do anything other than go after it.

And right then she knew what she wanted with that clearness of mind that only a condemned woman could have. She wanted to stay here, on this island, with this man, for whatever time she had left. Because no matter what he said or what tale he told, she knew she had met him that night near the lighthouse. And she knew he was the one she was meant to be with. She didn't know how it could be true. She didn't know what he was, exactly, only that he wasn't quite…normal. Wasn't quite…earthly. Or maybe…mortal.

And it was as that notion hit her that her gaze seemed drawn, almost of its own volition, to the corner of the cabin, way down low where the foundation met the earth. The solid square stones were fitted together perfectly, partially hidden by tall, graceful grasses and ornamental reeds. Still, she saw something in the stone and moved closer, frowning.

October, 1965.

How could that be? He'd said he'd built this place with his own hands. But he couldn't possibly have been here for more than forty-five years. He didn't look a day over thirty.

What the hell…?

She backed away, into the house, with a certain knowing settling into her. He wasn't mortal. But she wasn't dead. He wasn't an angel. He slept by day. He didn't seem to eat food.

Okay, just take a breath, she told herself. Just take a step back here and think on this. Could he be…something else? Something besides human?

That's ridiculous, Anna. It's just…

What if he was? What if he had the power to make her…that way, too? They could stay together then. She could be with him.

It hit her then, that rather than fear or disbelief her mind had jumped right to what had been her goal all along. Finding a way to stay with him. So staying with him was clearly what she wanted, what her heart desired. And she'd learned—from the man himself, in fact—that doing what her heart desired was the only way she wanted to live ever again. Dying or not.

The means to achieve that goal were just as clear: she had to make him *want* her to stay.

What if she was wrong, and he was just an ordinary man? What if the rest was all in her mind? Would it be fair to him to try to make him care for her when she was more than likely going to be dead in a few weeks?

But life was too short to always do what was best for others. He'd told her that. Or she thought he had. So she would spend her remaining time doing what was best for herself.

Besides, she'd told him her condition. He knew she was dying. He wouldn't be entering into anything unaware. She had to make inroads with the man. Somehow.

But he was so different from any man she'd ever known, she wasn't exactly sure how. So she watched him vanish around a bend in the trail, taking a fork they hadn't taken before, and then she went inside the house and explored it thoroughly. There really wasn't all that much to see. Very little food in the kitchen. Almost none. And while there were dishes in the cupboards, most of them wore a thin film of dust, as did the range. The fridge was the only appliance that appeared to be used regularly. Though it, too, was all but bare. Fresh fish, cleaned and ready to cook, lay in a glass dish with a tight-fitting plastic cover. But though the fridge looked well used, there was nothing else inside besides a pitcher of what looked like iced tea.

And the rest of the kitchen looked positively bereft.

How very odd.

There was no dining room, just a big archway that led back to the living room where she'd first awakened. Logs were stacked neatly beside the fireplace, and the room looked far more lived-in than the kitchen. A blanket lay over the back of a chair as if left there by someone who'd been enjoying its warmth. Books on wildlife and local vegetation lay here and there, one open, facedown, as if to hold its place.

Her eyes turned, drawn to the stairway, cleverly made of halved logs. She was pulled toward it, even though she sensed that she was dancing along the borderline of his tolerance. Even in her own mind, snooping was out of line. The bit she'd done so far seemed within an acceptable range, but as she walked up the stairs, she felt worse and worse.

She stood outside his bedroom door, her hand hovering near the antique brass doorknob that had the face of a bear engraved on it. But something stopped her. Something just wouldn't let her invade his privacy by sneaking into his bedroom. His sanctuary. It wouldn't be right.

Sighing, acknowledging inwardly her own disappointment in her willingness to pry, wondering what discoveries she might have made had she pressed on, she backed off and went instead to the very large bathroom that was the only other room on the second floor.

And she was glad she had.

The tub was a giant round Jacuzzi. Beside it, a shower stall twice as large as any she'd ever seen stood invitingly. She opened the etched glass door and saw that it was equipped with six showerheads at varying angles and heights. Wow.

The soaps and shampoos were mostly male-oriented, woodsy scents, or spicy ones. And her clothes, her own comfy pajamas, that she'd been wearing when the storm had tossed her little boat onto the rocks, were lying across a counter. They smelled of mild soap and fresh, ocean air. He'd washed them and hung them out to air-dry, she suspected.

All right, enough with the snooping. It was time to do some basking. Life was short, and there wasn't nearly enough basking being done by most of those living it. She ran the tub full of steaming hot water, which took far less time than she had expected. While it filled, she found several brand-new, still-wrapped toothbrushes in the nearby medicine cabinet and helped herself to one of them.

In short order she was soaking her bruised, battered limbs in the bubbling bath, head leaned back, eyes closed. She was exhausted from her little walk from the beach and her minuscule spying expedition. She'd really discovered very little, except that the man didn't seem to eat.

She was still very curious about him. But she

would just keep her eyes and ears open. She would ask him the things she wanted to know. She would look around some more when she had the chance, she told herself. Maybe even try to position herself close enough to the bedroom to get a glimpse inside when he opened the door.

Or maybe get herself invited in there in…some other way.

That idea appealed more than it ought to. Well, of course it did. She'd been dreaming of this man her entire life. Whether he believed it or not, she had. He was meant for her. Even if it was destined to last only a very little while.

She felt tears spring into her eyes at the notion of dying, of leaving him behind, and they were still burning there as she fell asleep.

She was in the house, though he would be damned if he could tell where. Her scent, however, that essence of Anna, was *everywhere*.

His houseguest had been snooping. The realization made his heart trip over itself, even though he had taken precautions. What if she had found something?

If she had, he asked himself, what was she going to do about it? Besides, hadn't he already suspected that she knew full well what he was?

That she was only pretending not to know? Playing him, the way Cassandra had?

His inner voice silenced that train of thought before he could ponder it through to the end. What she might do about it was hardly the point. His secrets were just that: *his,* meaning not hers to go digging around in. And *secrets,* meaning they were not for public knowledge. She had no right.

She wasn't in the living room, but her energy was. It was everywhere, on every shelf, in every corner. Not unpleasant, never that. Her essence was like a soft perfume, but more than a scent. It was her aura. Fragile, but fiery, like the tiny, spitting flame of a stubborn candle in a gentle rain.

And yes, he liked that about her.

But this was…too much. She'd touched his books, running her fingers over the spines as she'd skimmed the titles. She'd walked around the entire room, pausing near every shelf and painting, every stand and bauble, every heavily curtained and darkly shaded window. What had she made of those? he wondered. Heavy drapes of forest green, hanging over matching colored window shades, with shutters on the outside as an additional barrier against the sun. What had she thought about his need to completely shut out the daylight, assuming she didn't already know?

Her essence led him into the kitchen, where she had opened every cabinet and the refrigerator, too. Had she noticed the lack of food? Had she gone looking for what *really* kept him fed? He'd removed his bags of cold, clean human blood from the fridge only a few hours after he'd brought her here. He'd waited long enough to put warm, dry clothes on her, to cover her in blankets and build a fire nearby, to make sure she was going to live, then removed his stores of blood to the cooler out in the workshop.

Not finding Anna in the kitchen, he surged up the stairs, pausing where she had at his bedroom door. He felt the energy of her hand hovering near the doorknob and lowered his head in disappointment, before he realized that her essence ended there. She hadn't turned the knob or opened the door. The sense of her went no farther. She had not intruded into his bedroom. And not because he'd taken the precaution of locking her out. No. She hadn't even *tried* the door.

He felt a smile tug at the corners of his lips, felt the tension slowly ease from his body. His feelings of violation and resentment evaporated, and curiosity replaced them. What had stopped her?

And then a sneaking suspicion arose that caused the smile to falter. Had she simply run out of time? Had she heard him coming and had to scamper away, giving up on her day of prying into his shadows?

He lifted his head, turning and sensing her nearby, in the large bathroom that took up the other half of the second story. The door was ajar, far enough for him to see a naked, water-beaded knee in the tub. It wasn't moving. He stepped a little closer and saw more of her revealed. Her thigh vanished into the water, the sight of it blocked further by the tub itself. Her arm dangled over one side, long and slender and surprisingly toned for one so thin. But she'd been alone at sea for over a month, hadn't she? That would firm a person up, even a sick one.

And she *was* sick. He'd seen it before, the ravages of the antigen going to work on a mortal. Not in himself. He'd been turned before it got that bad, but he'd seen it in Cassandra. It was what had made him want to save her.

He banished that memory from his mind and moved a little closer, pushing the door wider now, but not quite going inside.

Anna was leaning back, her head tipped to rest against the edge of the tub. Her eyes were closed, mouth slightly open, hair bundled on top of her head, with curls cascading around her like a waterfall. As he stared, she inhaled and snorted a little.

His smile returned. No artifice there. She wasn't faking. She was truly asleep, and judging by the stillness of the water, the Jacuzzi jets, that ran for fifteen minutes before shutting themselves off and requiring you to hit the start button again, had long since gone silent. She'd been there awhile.

And that told him all he needed to know. She hadn't gone into his room because she had chosen not to. As curious as she must be, she'd chosen to respect his privacy.

For the first time, he considered that maybe she was genuine. Not a liar, like Cassandra. Not a user. Not a cold, calculating thief out to steal eternal life under false pretenses.

Maybe she was for real. As sweet and wonderful as she seemed.

And if he took one more step closer, he thought, he might see a whole lot more to like about the woman. But since she'd respected his privacy, though she obviously hadn't wanted to, he figured he ought respect hers in turn.

He backed out of the bathroom without so much as peeking at her body. Besides, he'd already seen it when he'd stripped off her sopping-wet clothes and dressed her in his own. And it wasn't a sight he was likely to forget. Not only because he hadn't glimpsed a naked woman in years, but because she was a beautiful specimen. A tempting one.

But he wasn't going to let his mind go in that direction.

He pulled the door closed, then knocked sharply, twice, to wake her. "Anna?" he called. "Are you in there?"

"Wha—oh!" There was a sloshing of water. "Yes, give me a minute."

"Of course."

More sloshing. Then the distinct sound of gurgling as the water started to drain. Moments later she was opening the door, holding one large plush towel around her torso, with another draped over her shoulders. Her hair was still up, wet tendrils dangling around her neck, and her face was sleepy. Leaning on the doorjamb, she smiled up at him. "I fell asleep in your tub. I'm sorry."

"It's perfectly all right. You're here to rest and to heal. Nothing to apologize for."

She nodded, but her eyes shot lower. "Not much healing that can be done, though. At least, not for what's really wrong."

"The weakness…it's getting worse?" he asked.

"I'm so sleepy all the time. I want to be exploring and playing and relishing what's left of my life, and particularly my time here on this beautiful island with you. But instead I'm falling asleep in the bathtub."

"There's a lot to be relished about a hot bath in an oversized Jacuzzi." He tipped his head slightly. "At least, as far as I recall from the last time I did so myself. You enjoyed it, yes?"

Her smile returned, as he had intended it to do. "Yes."

"Then no time was wasted. And there's still enough night left to enjoy. And since you so enjoyed the sunrise this morning…" He paused there, frowning at her. "You did, didn't you?"

"Not all of it." She lowered her head so that her curls fell damply across her cheek, then peered up at him from behind them with a sheepish grin. "I fell asleep *then,* too."

"Well, then, this will please you doubly. How about watching the moonrise instead?"

She frowned. "But it must be nearly…"

"Midnight," he filled in. "But it's a half-moon. They rise at midnight, set at midday, more or less. Very predictable, the moon."

"Yes, I love that about Her."

He lifted his eyebrows at her personification of the luminary, but other than that, let the comment go. "How quickly can you get dressed?"

"Five minutes."

"That fast?"

"What's to take time with?" she said, lifting the towel from her shoulders and using it to rub her hair. "It's warm outside, so there's not a lot to put on. Not to mention I've barely got any clothes to choose from, so making a selection won't take long."

"Well, we can remedy that. I noticed a few colorful items washing up on the shore, near where the boat's docked. Probably your clothes. Go on, get ready. I'll be waiting downstairs."

He turned to go, leaving her to it. And he wondered why he'd proposed what could be construed, he supposed, as a romantic evening together. Why would he put himself through that, take that risk, just because she had stopped herself from invading his privacy? Was it really all that impressive that she had managed not to do something that almost anyone would see as rude and unacceptable?

Given his experience with women in the past? Yes. It *was* that impressive.

Chapter 8

"Here we are." He nodded toward a tipped-over log that lay on the beach, just where the palm trees met the sand.

They were in a different spot from where she'd fallen asleep earlier. They'd circled the shoreline a little bit farther and come to a cozy cove where he'd built his own private dock.

"You can sit right there," he told her. "I've found that the log makes a comfortable back-rest."

But she didn't sit. She was too busy staring at the small sailboat tied to the pier he'd built in a tiny inlet where the water was shallow and mostly still. It was a small sailboat with a large motor attached, though its sails were tightly furled at the moment. The name *Santa Maria XIII* was painted in a beautiful, old-world-style script across the stern. She wondered about that *XIII*, even as she experienced a pang of longing for her own lost vessel. The feeling faded, though, as she noticed colorful items littering the shoreline. Frowning, she pointed. "Are those…?"

He smiled. "Your clothes and belongings have been washing up all evening. I spotted them earlier but wanted to check on you before coming down to gather them up."

"You spotted them…all the way from the house?"

"The workshop."

"That's a long way to see—especially in the dark. You must have very good eyesight." Suddenly her theory was seeming less and less ridiculous. Could he really be…? She couldn't even think the word.

"Excellent, in fact—particularly my night vision," he said.

She tried to hide her look of…well, shock, she supposed. Her crazy supposition was seeming more and more possible. To avoid his probing eyes, she started forward toward the debris on the shoreline, but he held up a hand. "I'll get them. You should rest."

"I'm fine at the moment, Diego. But thank you." She walked with him, and as the frothy surf washed over their bare feet she bent and began gathering up items she'd thought were long gone. A bikini top, no bottom in sight. A pair of denim shorts. A couple of tank tops and a T-shirt. She picked them up one by one, wringing them out as best she could and then draping them over one arm. She located one tennis shoe. A lot of good that was going to do her, she thought, when she failed to find its mate.

"It's better than nothing, though," he said, speaking as if in response to her thoughts. That was, of course, impossible.

Or was it?

When they'd picked up everything, she found herself closer to the little dock, and she studied his boat for a moment. "It's small," she said. "But nice."

"Wait until you see the new one," he said proudly.

"Don't tell me. The *Santa Maria...XIV?*"

He smiled, but didn't confirm it.

"Have there really been thirteen other boats,

Diego, or does the number mean something else?"

"I…are you sure you have all your clothes?"

"Just how long have you been here, Diego?"

He averted his eyes. "A long time."

"And you only go to the mainland…what did you tell me? Once a month?"

"Once a season, if I can manage it. But if supplies get low, I sometimes have no choice."

"I see. And when was the last time you went? For supplies, I mean."

"Just this past April. I was—" He stopped there, then began again. "Or it might have been March. I don't really keep track."

But she knew it had been April. April 10. The day she'd received her death sentence and gone to the shore to process the news. The day she'd met her guardian angel. And he'd been there, too. She knew it now for sure. She'd known it as soon as he'd said April, and he'd seen her know it, and then quickly tried to cover—to change his answer. But it was too late, and he knew it.

"It was you I met, you I kissed that night, wasn't it, Diego?"

He met her eyes again, held them. "Don't be ridiculous. How could it have been?"

She shrugged. "I guess you must be…some

kind of…supernatural being. You spoke to me mentally. You knew my name. You heard me crying out for help on the night of the storm. Didn't you?"

He lowered his head, saying nothing.

"How would it hurt you to tell me the truth, Diego? I'm dying, remember?"

He heaved a great sigh, then turned to focus on his small sailboat. "So what do you think of her?" he asked, changing the subject.

"I think she shouldn't be in the water. You don't leave her there all the time, do you?"

"Of course not. Only when a trip is imminent." He looked at her. "I put her in earlier tonight."

She blinked, afraid to ask why, but he answered, anyway.

"You'll be well enough to leave soon."

Was it too soon for her to ask him to let her stay? No. No, it was the right time, but she hadn't worked up enough courage to do it yet. Gnawing her lower lip and trying to compose a rational argument in her mind, she began walking through the warm sand, back toward the log where he'd suggested they sit. "I have a confession to make," she said softly, hoping to work her way up to what she really wanted to talk about.

"And what's that?"

She reached the log, curled her toes in the sand, then turned and sat down, getting comfortable and eyeing the horizon for the promised moonrise. Nothing in sight just yet, though. "I'm afraid I was a little nosy today. I kind of…looked around the house a little."

He nodded. "I know. You didn't go into my bedroom, however."

She felt her eyes widen. "How did you know?"

He shrugged. "Why didn't you go into my bedroom, Anna?"

She blinked, still blown away that he had known. "It would have been out of line," she said softly. "An invasion of your privacy. I just… It was outside my comfort zone, I guess."

"But looking around the rest of the place wasn't?"

"No." She lowered her eyes. "Maybe a little bit."

"So why did you?"

"I was curious. About you."

"I see. And did your explorations sate that curiosity?"

"No, not at all. If anything, they only sharpened it. The cornerstone of the cottage says 1965. How can that be, if you built it yourself?" She tipped her head to one side, waiting, expecting him to at least try to formulate an answer that made sense. But that wasn't what he did at all.

"I'm a very private man, Anna. That's probably obvious to you."

She blinked. "Well, yes. I mean, you live all alone on a deserted island. Can't get much more private than that. But...why? What made you want to live this way?"

He looked away. "I can't help but wonder what part of the word *private* you don't understand?"

"You're being mean now."

He looked back at her. "Sorry."

"It was a woman, wasn't it?"

He rolled his eyes and walked closer, but passed her to bend down near the log. He pulled out a bottle of wine and two glasses, then filled one to the brim and handed it to her.

"Nice," she said. "Aren't you having any?"

"Of course," he said. And then he filled his own glass, sank into the sand beside her, leaned back against the log and pointed. "Look, here it comes."

She fell silent, though her questions were still screaming in her mind. She shut her lips tightly, determined to enjoy this night to the fullest.

Relaxing there, she sipped the wine, which was delicious, and leaned back and watched the moon climb into the sky, lopsided and a bit less than half-formed, rising slowly above the water and sending a long beam outward, like a glowing arrow pointing straight from the moon to this very stretch of beach. Pointing right at her. At them.

"That's amazing. So beautiful," she said.

"I agree."

His words were soft and his eyes, she found when she looked his way, were on her. Not the moon.

"Diego," she whispered. "I won't be here very long."

"I know."

"And I won't snoop anymore."

"That's good to hear."

"But I want..." She got lost in his eyes. There was a passion in them that was beyond anything she'd seen before. A desire she'd never seen focused on her. "I want you," she whispered, even though it wasn't what she had intended to say at all.

"That would be a mistake," he told her.

She smiled broadly. "How could it be? I've got nothing to lose, Diego. I'm dying. And my guardian angel told me to do exactly what I wanted to do with the time I had left. And what I want to do right now is kiss you. And so I'm going to."

She leaned up, and he didn't pull away. Her lips moved close to his, then, boldly, pressed against them. He remained motionless as she slid her hands over his shoulders and around to the back of his neck, then threaded her fingers into his hair and held him to her so she could press harder, kiss deeper.

She felt him shudder, and then he gave in. He wound his arms around her waist and bent over her, pushing her back into the sand so that his body was angled over hers, and then he kissed her. He kissed her like she'd never been kissed before, and every single part of her came alive.

"Diego," she whispered. "Diego."

She arched upward against him, felt the hardness of his arousal pressing into her thigh. And then, to her stunned amazement, he rolled away, sitting up, blinking in the night as if his entire being were shattered.

"Diego?" she asked.

He said nothing. She sat up, as well, sliding a hand over his shoulders from behind.

"Please, talk to me."

"There's nothing to talk about. I can't do this with you, Anna. I know where it's going to end, and I don't want to go there again."

She closed her eyes. "I want to stay here, Diego. I want to stay here, on the island with you, for whatever time I have left in this life. It can't be more than a month—six weeks at the outside."

"No." It sounded as if he had to force the word through a space too tight for it.

"But…but I'm dying. I don't have anything to go back to. I'll stay out of your way, I'll do whatever you need me to do, but please, don't make me go back."

He rose to his feet, so that her hands fell from his broad shoulders. She stayed where she was. "You need to leave. And you're obviously strong enough to do so. We'll set sail tomorrow night at sundown."

"Diego, please!"

"Don't beg, Anna. It's beneath you."

"I don't have a damn thing to lose."

"There's always your pride."

"You're a hard, cold man, aren't you?"

He shrugged. "I'm going to my workshop for a few hours. I don't want to be bothered."

"Fine. You go to your damn workshop, you selfish bastard."

He walked away, seemingly unperturbed by her parting shot. Anna sank to her knees in the sand and wept bitterly. And she wasn't even sure why.

Chapter 9

She sat there in the sand, staring out at the half-moon and drinking the bottle of wine he'd left behind. When she was all cried out, she sat in silence for a while, trying to analyze just what was behind her roiling feelings. They were confused and tumultuous, far from the peaceful, blissful state she'd found while alone at sea.

That state, she decided, had been one of calm acceptance. She knew she was dying. She had made a choice to spend her time on the sea, and she had been enjoying every moment of it.

That was no longer the case, and she struggled to figure out why. Why, for example, wasn't her dying request to Diego something entirely different? Why wasn't she begging him to loan her his sailboat so that she could continue on the path she had chosen, to die at sea, maybe sail close to this island again when she sensed the time was near and just anchor offshore, so he could come get his boat when it was over?

That request would have made more sense to her. To him, too, probably. But she had no desire to borrow his boat or head back out to sea. Her only wish was to stay here on this tiny chunk of paradise. And not alone, either. She wanted to stay here with *him*. There was something so... so compelling about him. Something that felt... intimately connected to her. She wanted to touch him, to be close to him all the time, and she barely knew the man. And yet it felt as if she knew him. It felt as if she'd known him all her life.

And loved him even longer.

She was no longer so much at peace with dying. Rather than that calm, blissful state of acceptance she'd felt before, there was now a sense of time running out. A sense of urgency to use what time was left to get closer to him, to this place.

She closed her eyes, lowered her head and

sighed. Maybe it was just the approach of her own end making her feel such a wild array of nonsensical emotions. Maybe everyone got all tied up in knots when they knew they were short on time. Of course they did. Why wouldn't they?

Okay, so she needed to get a handle on this. Probably apologize to him, and maybe try to explain what had led to her outburst. And then she would get back to the task at hand, convincing him to let her stay. Because no matter what he said, she had no intention of leaving. He would have to carry her bodily off this island if he wanted to get rid of her. Whether to tell him that, too, was still up in the air in her mind.

She opened her eyes, feeling better, empowered, calm, resolved, and found herself focusing on a stain in the white sand.

A red stain. Like blood.

It was right beside the spot where Diego had been sitting, on the side of him that had been farthest from her. She frowned, bending closer, wondering if he'd been injured and unaware of it, or—

And then she saw the wineglass, sitting empty on the log, and knew it wasn't blood. That stain was wine. She bent closer, sniffed. Yes, it was wine. He'd poured himself a glass, but as her mind replayed the events of the past hour, she realized she had never actually seen him take a single sip of it.

And in her mind she heard the actor Bela Lugosi in the role that had made him famous, saying, in his thick Romanian accent, "I never drink...wine."

"Oh, come on, Anna," she said aloud. "Just cut it out, already." And yet her eyes were glued to that stain in the sand.

She shifted her gaze to look out at the moonlight beaming down on the water, as perfectly beautiful as if it were the backdrop on a movie set. And her mind kept on taunting her. *He's nocturnal. He said so himself. And you've certainly never seen him in the daylight.*

"He hasn't seen *me* in the daylight, either," she argued.

No food in the house. And not just curtains on the windows, but heavy drapes, and window shades, and shutters to boot.

"Just because he doesn't like the sun, doesn't mean..."

You've got to get a look inside that bedroom.

But then her thoughts ground to a sudden halt, as she heard him cry out in what sounded like pain. She was on her feet, turning toward the path back and even starting forward, before she realized she hadn't heard the shout with her ears.

She'd heard it with her mind.

And she felt it still, that sense of him, hurting and in distress, ringing in her head, a feeling, not a sound. She was compelled to go to him. She dropped her wineglass beside the empty bottle in the sand and ran.

He'd been careless. Angry, frustrated, stupid and careless. Because he wanted so very badly to believe her when she told him she wanted to stay on this island…to stay with him. But he'd been told the same thing before. By a woman in the very same circumstances.

He'd taken his angst out on his work, and now the circular saw lay on the floor, its teeth clinging to bits of his flesh, and his forearm was gushing blood at a pace that would kill him in very short order.

"Oh, my God! Diego!"

And then she was there on the floor beside him, and acting without any kind of hesitation or panic or delay. She looked around, assessed the situation and sprang into action, grabbing a box cutter from his workbench and quickly slicing the power cord off the saw. Kneeling beside him, she wrapped the cord around his arm, above the gash, then knotted it once, tightly. Getting up again, she grabbed a big screwdriver and laid the blade atop the cord, then knotted the cord again over the blade to create an instant tourniquet. She twisted the screwdriver, tightening the cord around his arm, and he couldn't help but cry out in pain.

She shot him a look—and he saw tears welling in her eyes. One spilled over and rolled slowly down her cheek. "Don't die," she said.

He couldn't look away. "I…tend to bleed like… like a hemophiliac," he explained. "It's not going to clot."

"I'm the same way," she told him, wonder at that in her eyes, and then she pushed her questions aside. "I can stitch it up."

He shook his head. "The pain—I have a very low threshold for pain."

"Then what? We can't just leave the tourniquet on indefinitely. You'll lose your arm."

"What time is it?"

"What earthly difference does *that* make?"

"Please…"

She shrugged. "About three-thirty, but I'm only guessing."

"Two hours, then."

"Until what?"

"Sunrise," he told her.

She looked at him sharply, holding his head in her lap now. "And what happens at sunrise, Diego?"

He averted his eyes, but he'd heard the knowing in her voice. She'd either known what he was all along or she was beginning to figure it out. "If you can help me back to the house, get me to my room, I'll be fine."

"Before sunrise, right? I have to get you to your bed before sunrise? And then you'll be fine?"

"Yes."

She tipped her head to one side, staring at him, and he saw her deciding not to press him for the truth. Not now, at least, when he was in imminent danger from a cut that shouldn't have been all that serious. And *certainly* shouldn't have bled as much as it had. He saw her looking at the amount of blood on the floor around him, and he read her thoughts almost without trying.

"You're going to have to tell me sometime," she said softly. "But at least now you won't be in any condition to make me leave tomorrow night." She pulled his uninjured arm around her shoulders and got to her feet, helping him to rise with her.

His knees nearly buckled beneath him, and she got a better grip around his waist and said, "Diego, this is worse than it ought to be. It's not that bad a cut."

"It's the blood loss. And the pain. If I make it till morning, I'll be all right."

"Right. If you make it till morning." He looked bad. He looked worse than bad, he looked near death, she thought.

They walked—stumbled, really—together to the house, and she got him inside. Somehow they managed to get up the stairs, and at his bedroom door he paused, leaning on the wall as if it was all he could do to remain standing.

"Key…in my pocket."

Nodding, she thrust a hand into the pocket of his khaki trousers and felt around, finding the key and pulling it out, and quickly unlocking the bedroom door. Then she helped him inside, into utter blackness.

"I was dying to get a look in here," she told him. "But not like this." Her attempt at levity fell flat, though. They shuffled forward through inky darkness, and then he fell onto a bed that she hadn't even seen. She leaned over him, feeling around to get her bearings. She got him straightened out as best she could. Then, holding her hands in front of her, she made her way back to the open door, guided by the light that came from beyond it, and found, as she had expected, a light switch just inside the doorway. She flipped it on and turned for her first glimpse of his bedroom.

And then she blinked, because it was just an ordinary bedroom, with one notable exception. "There are no windows," she said softly. She looked at him, lying there on the bed. "Why are there no windows, Diego?"

He didn't answer. He was lying still, and his skin was startlingly pale. She hurried to the bed, climbed onto it beside him, kneeling there, her hands on his shoulders. "Diego? Diego, just tell me what to do—please."

He opened his eyes to mere slits. "I… need…"

"What? Tell me what you need and I'll get it for you. Just tell me. Diego? Diego, what is it?"

He stared at her, trying hard to keep his eyes focused, she thought, but she could see the pupils dilating and contracting over and over.

"I'm dying," he said.

"No! No, Diego, you are *not*. Tell me what to do. *Tell me*."

He tipped his head back as his eyes widened in a burst of pain and his mouth opened wide, and she saw his incisors. She jumped from the bed, moving backward away from it, but only three steps. And then she stopped herself, swallowed hard, stood still, staring at him. "My God, it's true. I've been thinking it all night, but I just didn't think it was possible. You're…you're…"

"A vampire," he whispered. "But you already knew, didn't you? Isn't that why you came?"

She frowned. "You're talking crazy now. It's the blood loss, I guess." She swallowed and moved close to him again. "You saved my life, Diego," she whispered. "And I know you're the one who spoke to me that night so long ago. It seems like forever. But I know it was you. You're the reason I took what time I had left to do what I wanted. You're the reason I'm even here." Lifting her chin, she nodded once, firmly, unsure whether he was even hearing her. And it didn't matter. She was talking mostly to herself, anyway.

She moved to the bed, put one knee up on the mattress, then the other, and leaned close to him.

"I'm dying, anyway. I have nothing to lose. Take what you need, Diego. Take it from me."

He opened his eyes and met hers again, and his were glowing now, glowing from somewhere within, glowing and sort of…feral. It was frightening, and yet she couldn't look away. Lifting her hand, she reached behind her head to pull her hair around to one side. She slid her other hand beneath his head to lift it gently from the pillows as she bent even closer. His cool lips brushed against the warm skin of her neck. Taking a breath, then another, she closed her eyes, bracing herself. His mouth parted, and his hands slid upward to gently cup the back of her head. Then his grip turned fierce, and he bit down with a growl that reverberated right to her soul.

Chapter 10

He was lost. Lost in a red haze of ecstasy, of healing, of hunger and of desire. Lost until the luscious elixir that rejuvenated his life force and alleviated his pain finally got around to clearing his head. Only slightly, though. Yes, feeding kept him alive and eased the pain that was dulling his mind. But it replaced that fog with the bloodlust, which was nearly as mindless.

With the force of sheer will, he withdrew his razor-sharp incisors from her butter-soft skin and lifted his head.

She stared at him, her eyelids heavy with the opiate effect of the vampire's kiss and the heavy weight of passion that went hand in hand. In his kind, feeding and sex were urges that were intertwined, and sating one fed the need to sate the other. In the victims, it was very similar. Sharing blood was an act as intimate as—no, more intimate than—intercourse. It was powerful.

As he stared into her beautiful eyes, he wanted her.

And then, drunk with the act he had just committed, she whispered, "Please?"

He blinked against his own aching need, shook his head, pushed her from him. "No."

But she gripped the hem of her blouse and tugged it over her head. Her breasts bounced as the fabric released them, round and full and soft. "I need you," she told him.

And then she leaned over him again, her lips meeting his, opening, suckling his lips and teasing with her tongue. "I've *always* needed you…"

He didn't have a choice. He wasn't made of stone. He was a creature of passions, for God's sake. Blood and sex and life were all blended together in him, and there was just no way to avoid this. He'd never wanted, never *needed,* like this before. Never.

Not even with Cassandra.

He wrapped his arms around Anna and returned her kiss, and it felt as if the fires of hell itself rose up and wrapped around them.

And then it felt like heaven instead.

Her mind vanished, and all that remained was her body, her senses. And pleasure, mind-blowing pleasure that left her quivering and weak. But gradually, very, very gradually, she came back to herself and realized that she was lying naked in his arms, and that she'd just had hours of passionate sex with a man who'd been near death.

No, not a man.

A vampire.

Her mind didn't want to wrap itself around that, but there was no other way to explain what… She raised her hand and pressed it against the skin of her neck. Yes, there were wounds there. Puncture wounds, two of them, tiny, swollen and tender.

He'd admitted the truth. And if that hadn't been enough, he'd bitten her neck.

He'd drunk of her blood.

He was a vampire.

Blinking and waiting for that truth to sink in,

to make sense, she decided at length that it never would. She didn't feel afraid of him. She didn't feel any need to run away. In fact, she felt…she felt better than she had before. He'd shown her his true self. He'd let her into his lonely world.

For whatever time she had, she would embrace this new reality. What difference did it make, when she would be dead herself in a few weeks' time?

She sat up a little, propped her tired head on her hand and smiled down at him. He didn't smile back. He lay very still. *Very* still.

"Diego?"

She touched him. "Diego, are you all right?" And then, when he still didn't respond, she shook his shoulder. "Diego, wake up!"

But there was no response.

God, she'd killed him! She'd become so lost in passion that they must have knocked the tourniquet loose and—

Even as she thought it, she turned to inspect his arm. The tourniquet was still in place, but the wound…the wound was…it was vanishing.

She blinked her eyes, rubbed them, then leaned closer, staring at something that couldn't possibly be real. The cut in his arm was mending itself, the skin pressing together in a kiss and sealing itself. In minutes there was only a faint red line remaining, and even that faded before her eyes, growing paler by degrees.

Carefully, her heart in her throat, she loosened the tourniquet and then stared hard at the arm. There was no more bleeding. How could there be, when there was no cut?

If I make it till morning, I'll be all right.

She guessed it must be morning, then. And by day, it seemed, his wounds healed. But even stranger was that fact that he certainly didn't seem alive right now. He seemed like a corpse. Except, not stiff. And not cold, either. In fact, he felt warmer than he had since she'd been here.

Slowly, she slid out of the bed and stood staring down at him. Should she check for a heartbeat? Did vampires even have one? How could she tell if he were alive or dead? Or undead? How could she know?

Blinking, she backed away. All right, she would just have to wait for nightfall, then, wouldn't she? That would tell the tale. She would wait for nightfall. And he would wake. Or not.

And if he didn't, then she supposed…she would have to bury him.

Tears welled in her eyes and spilled over, and she rushed back to the bed, flung herself onto it and wrapped her arms around him. "Don't be dead, Diego! Please don't be dead! I don't care what you are. You gave me my life. You *did*. You convinced me to *live,* for the first time, for the only time, with the tiny bit of time I have left. And I am so grateful to you for that. You really are my guardian angel, even if some people would call you a demon. And I don't want to lose you now. Not now. So please, don't be dead, Diego. Please?"

She wept harder than she had ever wept before, even that day in Mary's office. And eventually she fell asleep there, her head on his chest, her arms linked around his shoulders, sobs racking her body every few minutes even then. She slept hard for what amounted to most of the day.

By the time she roused, it was well after 7:00 p.m. Being summer, sundown wouldn't come for a couple more hours yet. And he was still unresponsive, but since it wasn't yet dark, there was still hope. In fact, with his arm showing no sign it had ever been injured at all, she had more hope than before.

She was refreshed and feeling absurdly good. He would wake up. He had to.

She couldn't seem to stop smiling. And her

attitude was so positive that she couldn't *wait* for Diego to wake so she could share another perfect, blissful night with him. In the meantime she decided to kill time as best she could. She started with a glorious hot shower, lavishing herself with the best-smelling soaps in his overstocked bathroom.

She got creative then, bundling her hair up on top of her head but leaving it loose enough that curling tendrils spilled around her like a crown of spiral silk. She made a sarong from a nearly sheer silk throw, in a French vanilla cream color that she thought was the height of romance. She searched the house for candles, lined his bedroom with them, and set a lighter nearby. And then, with around half an hour to go, she realized she was half-starved, so she filled her belly with fruits from the island, downed a glass of icy cold water, brushed her teeth and returned to the bedroom.

She lit all the candles, and then she tried to strike an alluring pose near one of them as she waited for him to rouse.

Minutes ticked by. And then more minutes. She began to fear he might really be dead, after all.

But finally his nose twitched. And then it wrinkled.

Suddenly he sat up fast, eyes flying wide, and shouted, "Fire!"

"No!" She hurried to the bed and put her hands on his shoulders. "No, Diego, it's just candles. There's no fire."

He scanned the room, wild-eyed, and bounded from the bed without even looking at her, then stood there staring at the tiny flames that surrounded him. And then, finally, his gaze found hers and a little of the wildness faded.

She smiled, relieved. "Thank God," she said, sliding from the bed. "I wasn't sure if you were going to wake up or not. I mean, when you sleep, it's as though—but then the cut, it healed, and so… Oh, I'm just so glad you're alive, Diego. So glad." She moved closer to him as she spoke, and by the end she was sliding her hands up over his shoulders and resting her head on his chest.

He put his hands on her shoulders, as well, but didn't wrap his arms around her as she had expected him to do. He seemed tentative. Probably just hadn't caught up with himself yet. When you slept that deeply, you must wake up a little disoriented, right? He needed to process everything, to remember the night before, to—

"I need you to put the candles out, Anna. I'd do it myself, but I could easily go up in flames without a snuffer, so…"

"Go up in flames?" She lifted her head, because he didn't *sound* confused or disoriented.

"After last night, I suppose there's no longer any question in your mind about what I am."

She smiled shyly, lowering her eyes even as she lifted her palm to press it to the marks on her neck. But then she frowned. "They're gone," she whispered, her eyes flying to his.

"They heal at the first touch of sunlight."

"Oh. Just like your injuries do."

"Mine heal during the day sleep. The touch of sunlight would be a whole different problem for me."

"I see. And fire?"

"My kind are highly flammable. I only keep a supply of candles on hand in case my power sources fail and light is needed."

"I didn't know," she said. "I'm sorry…about the candles." She quickly went around the room, blowing them out one by one until they stood in total darkness, the scent of smoldering wicks and hot wax too much to bear.

He opened the bedroom door. "Have you eaten?" he asked.

"Yes, I…I'm fine. Full. Thank you."

"Good. The journey will only take about four hours. Giving me ample time to get back before sunrise, but only if we leave within the next—"

"Journey?"

He stopped at the foot of the stairs, turning to look up at her. "Back to the mainland. Did you forget I was taking you back tonight?"

She blinked rapidly, her heart taking the blow that felt like a blade straight through it. Her throat constricted, and though she opened her mouth to reply, she couldn't force out a sound.

"Why don't you…" His eyes moved down her makeshift outfit, that had felt like a seductress's peignoir before and now felt like a silk throw. "Change," he finished.

"I…I thought…after last night…what we shared…"

"It was the bloodlust, Anna." He looked away when he said it, unable to hold her eyes, she thought, probably because he knew he was being a coldhearted bastard. "When a vampire feeds from a living being, sexual desire is…one of the side effects. It's nearly irresistible."

She blinked, her eyes burning with tears. "That's all it was? It would have happened… with anyone?" she asked.

"No, not with anyone. But with any beautiful woman, probably, yes, it would have happened."

"Then it meant nothing," she said softly.

"It didn't mean what you want it to mean. Can we leave it at that?"

She was silent for a moment, but inside, way down deep where he couldn't see—or could he? She was burning with anger, humiliation and rage.

"I gave you my blood," she said softly. "And I gave you my body. And you won't even give me a few weeks on your precious island before I die?"

He lowered his head. "I will visit you again before you die," he told her. "And I'll repay your favor at that time. But until then, it's best you go."

Blinking rapidly, she lowered her head. "All right, then."

Suddenly it felt as if someone were poking around inside her brain. Her head snapped up, and she found his eyes on her, the intensity in them telling her that he was doing *something*. Trying to read her thoughts? So she filled her mind with the image of walking along the beach, saying goodbye to the island.

"If you don't mind," she said softly, "I'd like a

few minutes alone. I'm going down to the beach. I'll gather up any more of my things that might have washed up today."

He seemed to relax a little, and he nodded. "That's a good idea. I need to pack a few things for the trip, anyway. I'll meet you at the boat in… half an hour?"

She nodded and headed back up the stairs to his bedroom, where she pulled her clothes on as fast as she could, then grabbed the lighter from the nightstand and tucked it into her pocket.

She was staying on this island. She was staying for the rest of her life. As near as she could figure, that might be another four to six weeks. So she was staying. Whether her guardian vampire liked it or not.

Chapter 11

It was killing him to treat her as coldly as he was. He didn't want to. He wanted to scoop her right up off her feet and carry her back to bed. He wanted to ravish her over and over. He wanted to drink from her again. He wanted to feed her, too. Feed her from his own veins. Share the Gift with her.

But what he wanted had nothing to do with anything. Self-preservation came first. It was what had brought him to this island in the first place. The need to stay solitary. The need to be completely self-contained and not dependent upon anything temporal. And everything was

temporal, when you came down to it. Everything.
Humans, totally mortal. Lived, died, gone.
Houses, homes, rotted with time. Cars fell apart.
Money. Jobs. Hobbies. Friends. Relationships,
even with other immortals. Nothing lasted.

Nothing but him.

He was meant to be alone. He'd lost sight of
that for a time with Cassandra. But he'd learned
from that experience, from the pain of it. And
he'd brought himself around to being at peace
with solitude again. Until Anna had shown up
here and brought all those old longings back to
screaming life.

If she stayed any longer, he was going to fall in
love with her. He was going to let himself believe
she really was everything she seemed. Already
he felt himself sliding down that slippery path.
How many times, just in the past hour, had he
caught himself believing in her?

Why was it so hard to let her—make her—go?

She was one of the Chosen. All right. He got
that. That meant that there was an automatic
bond between them. He couldn't hurt her, not
even if he wanted to. And he was compelled to
help, to protect, to watch over her. He got that,
too. Those things were the case with any member
of her caste.

But this…this feeling of her being…being a part of him, of his life, of his soul, a part that had been missing all this time—it made no sense. It was far beyond what he'd come to understand were the limits of the blood link between his kind and hers.

The sharing of blood increased the power of the bond. He knew that, too. But he'd had little choice about drinking from her. He would have died otherwise. But that had only made things worse. Made her feel even more a part of him. A necessity to him.

Probably he was suffering some ordinary reaction brought on by spending years with almost zero contact with other living beings. Probably it was natural to imagine some supernatural bond with the first female to come stumbling into his life in nearly half a century.

But it wasn't good for him to feel this way. He wasn't going to humor this thing, or even tolerate it. She had to go before he fell any harder for her.

As he thought that, he realized he was actually afraid of her. Afraid of the heartbreak she could cause, of his own vulnerability, of the pain he'd suffered the last time. He, Diego del Torres, who'd sailed aboard the *original Santa Maria*, an immortal, a vampire, was afraid of a small mortal female who'd lived only a few decades.

And no, he told himself, he wasn't going to just let her die. He was going to monitor her condition. He would know how she was doing. This link between them was that powerful—even more so now that he'd tasted her blood. When she got near the end, he would go to her. He would tell her there was an option, let her make the choice.

But he wasn't going to put his heart on the line for her. Or for anyone.

They say no man is an island. But they're wrong—this man is.

He returned to his task of packing a bag for the trip to the mainland. A change of clothes, first-aid kit, toothbrush. He needed a pint of frozen blood, and he'd moved his supply to the cooler in the workshop, to keep her from finding it. Not that it mattered now. As soon as he returned and she was gone, he would move his stores back where they belonged.

When she was gone.

The notion made his heart contract into a hard, painful knot in his chest. Already, he thought, she was causing him pain. If he needed any more proof that he was doing the right thing in sending her away, that was it. Things would only get worse if he let her stay.

I'm going to miss her.

Yes, but only at first. He would get over it, and soon he would be comfortable again. Happy again.

Happy? Again? When have I ever been truly happy?

"Silence," he said to the voice that seemed to be coming more from his heart than his head. He slung his bag over his shoulder and headed for the front door, intent on reaching the workshop and the blood stored there. But as soon as he opened the door he smelled and tasted the acrid burn of smoke on the air, felt the blast of her anger. If he hadn't been so self-absorbed, he would have sensed both far sooner.

He dropped his satchel and ran full speed to the cove, following that sense of her all the way there, stopping when he caught sight of her. She was standing in the shallows, her back to him, watching the *Santa Maria XIII* go up in flames. The fire licked at the night sky with a hunger that rivaled any he'd ever felt.

He stopped in his tracks, too stunned to move, anger surging in him that rivaled hers. "Anna!" he shouted. "What the hell have you done?"

She didn't turn, just stood where she was, feet in the surf, watching the fire leap and dance. The heat of it seared his face, and dangerous sparks rained down around him. "Fire is so beautiful, isn't it?" she at last said softly.

"Why did you do this?" Her refusal to answer his questions made him even angrier, so he strode up behind her, gripped her shoulder and spun her around to face him. "*Why*, Anna?"

"You didn't leave me any choice, Diego."

There were tears streaming down both her cheeks. And his heart seemed to crack a bit, the inside softening, as if the heart of the fire were actually penetrating it. But it wasn't the fire prying its way into his heart, and he knew it.

"The choice was to go," he said. "This is *my* island, Anna. It's my life you're intruding on. You have no right." His hands on her shoulders were tight, might even have seemed menacing, had his tone not had the distinct ring of a condemned man pleading for mercy, he thought. He didn't *sound* menacing. Nor did he feel that way.

"What are you going to do, Diego? You going to hurt me? Or drain me dry and finish this once and for all?"

He bared his teeth in a flash of temper, wishing he could oblige her, but knowing better. He gave her a slight shove as he let go, then paced in a circle, furious.

"It's not in you to hurt me, Diego. We both know that. There's something…something between us."

"I drank from you. That gives you the sense that we have a bond, but it's just an illusion," he argued. "It's chemistry. Nothing more."

"I saved your life last night. And I gave you something more precious to me than that blood you so desperately needed."

"I didn't ask for that."

"You didn't turn it down, either. And whether you admit it or not, you felt something, Diego. More than chemistry, more than physical lust and release, more than any kind of blood bond. You felt something. I know you did. I was there. Why are you trying so hard to deny it?"

"Because it's not what I want."

She clenched her jaw, and her eyes flashed with impatience, with temper, and with what he thought was the first hint of certainty. She thought he was weakening.

And God help him, he was.

"I want to spend the last weeks of my life here, in this place. This is where I want to die."

"And what about what *I* want?" he demanded,

already knowing she had defeated him. Because what could he possibly do now? His only means of transportation was gone. Destroyed, by her hand.

She shrugged. "You're immortal, right?" Turning, she stared at the boat again. "You've got plenty of time to have what you want."

"This is unforgivable," he said. "It's unfathomable that you would go to such lengths to get your way."

"Refusing to let me stay is what's unforgivable, Diego. Especially after…" She stopped there, then waved a hand at the burning sailboat. "This… this is barely even bad. It wasn't that great a boat. You've got a gorgeous one taking shape in your workshop, so it's not as if I'm marooning you out here. You said it would be finished in a few more weeks. By then I'll be dead. And you'll be rid of me." She turned to look him in the eyes. "Until then, you're just going to have to tolerate my presence."

She was hurting. He could feel it in her, practically screaming way down inside. It wasn't anger, as he'd initially thought. It was pain. That flaming boat in front of him right now was no more than the visual evidence of her pain, scorching its way into the sky.

He lowered his head, wondering if he were the cause of all that pain. "Why are you hurting so much?"

"Why? Because I'm dying, you idiot. I'm *dying.* I thought I'd made peace with that, but that was when I thought I had this wonderful, beautiful, wise and ageless guardian angel waiting for me on the other side. But then I come here, and I find—" She bit her lip. "Never mind. Just go finish your stupid boat. And if you finish it before I breathe my last, I'll go. All right?"

He nodded slowly, but he was trying to read more into her words, trying to see the feeling behind them. There was something trying to make its way from the sublevels of his mind, some knowing that he hadn't let himself hear or see before. He felt it. It was knocking on his awareness. "I'll…go work on it now," was all he could think of to say.

"Yeah, you do that. Try not to cut off your arm this time." And with that she stomped away from him, heading along the shoreline, her pace rapid, her posture angry.

His fists clenched and unclenched at his sides as he watched her go; he felt utterly helpless in his anger and confusion. He turned to stare at the fire, and then tipped his head back and released an anguished shout at the heavens. Why had the gods seen fit to disrupt his peaceful, perfect, solitary existence with *her?*

She walked along the beach, gathering up more of her possessions as she did. A hairbrush, twined full of seaweed. A useless wiry tangle of algae and headphones that had gone with her MP3 player. A book.

She bent and picked it up. Soggy pages, but intact, waterproof ink still legible. It was her journal, the one she'd been keeping since the day she'd found out her diagnosis, the day she'd set sail. She felt compelled to keep it, so she carried it back to the house with her and patted it dry with a thick towel. Then she lit the oven, setting it on the lowest temperature, and set the journal inside, open facedown.

Every five minutes or so she turned the pages, and the process seemed to be working. In between, she hand-washed all the clothing she'd scavenged from the beach, then hung each item outside, making use of every tree branch and bush she could find.

As she worked, the birds of the night sang to her, and she paused to just close her eyes and listen to them. Their voices, their songs, seemed full of hope, and the ocean sound beyond them, that gentle whisper of waves washing over sand, an almost inaudible message. They were speaking to her. She was sure of it. Saying her name. Telling her it was all going to be okay. And the stars, glittering above, spelled out the same message in some kind sparkly code. *It's all fine. Everything's okay. Just relax and be easy about all of this. It's fine.*

She stood there listening, trying to hear with her heart the words being spoken to her by nature. And yet her heart ached. She closed her eyes and let the night wind caress her face, but her cheeks burned from the rivers of tears flowing over them. "How can it be okay when I've found the man of my dreams, only to make him hate me? How can it be okay when I've landed in a paradise that can never be mine? How can everything ever be okay when I've found my heart's desire just in time to die and leave it all behind?"

Suddenly her body felt very light. As if she were no longer even inside it. That empty body fell to the sand like a suit without a wearer, and this time it was different from the tiredness she'd felt before, the weakness, the need to sleep. This felt like being taken to a whole new level.

This was, she thought, the end.

Weakly, she lifted her hand and started to drag her forefinger through the warm sand.

Chapter 12

He spent a couple of hours working on what was now his only means of transportation, all the while working through things in his mind. He was trying to make sense of everything bit by bit, and he was still certain she was in the wrong. She was forcing him to do what he didn't want to do, and she'd had no right. It was his life, his island, his boat.

But she seemed to feel she had every right, just because she only had a few weeks left to live. The thing was, that wasn't true. She could live forever if she wanted to. She just didn't know that. Because he hadn't told her.

Why not? he wondered.

He knew the answer. He feared her reaction would be the same as Cassandra's had been. She would accept his offer, declaring her utter delight that they could stay together, after all. And then he would transform her. And then she would leave him.

But, finally, the distant knowledge that had been waiting patiently beyond the doorway of his subconscious managed to slip inside.

Why would that bother you? You've been trying to get her to leave, after all. Why not change her and let her go?

"Because I don't want to be used again, taken advantage of again, lied to again."

Or is it because you don't want to be proven right about her? That you want to believe in her?

He shook his head. "No. No, it's not that at all. I want her out of here before I can fall in love with her, then have my heart broken again. That's all."

But don't you see, Diego? It's already too late for that.

He blinked in stunned surprise at the revelation he'd been denying, closing his eyes to, refusing to see. He already loved her.

He already loved her.

So if she left, either by her own volition or by his order, he was doomed to suffer that heartache again, anyway. There was no way around it.

He had been dreading rejection by yet another beautiful woman to whom he'd offered all he had to offer. He'd been living his entire life in an elaborate design to prevent that very thing from ever happening.

And yet Anna had found him. She'd found his haven, despite all his precautions. And she'd found a way into his heart, despite all his fortifications. Maybe there was something here that deserved a deeper look. Maybe she'd been nothing more than honest with him the entire time.

What about that?

He pondered and nodded, understanding her anger a bit more. From her point of view, he could see how unreasonable he must seem to deny her dying wish. It was only a few weeks, from her perspective. It must seem very selfish to her for him to say no, and so adamantly, too. Especially after last night.

Yes, that must really have added fuel to her fire, he thought, seeing again his burning boat in his mind's eye. No wonder she'd done what she had. She must feel just as rejected as…as he'd been fearing he would feel if he gave her the Gift, and his heart along with it, and she walked away.

Exactly like that, he realized. She'd given him her blood. Her body. Her heart, perhaps. She'd saved his life. And he'd thrown her precious gift back in her face, rejected her. He'd done to her, he realized in dawning horror, exactly what Cassandra had done to him.

The revelation made him stop sanding and rise to his feet. Damn, that was it. He needed to apologize. Maybe even offer an explanation, if she were still willing to listen. And he needed to tell her the truth about her nature, her condition, what it all meant.

He tuned in to her, though he'd been tuning her out for the past two hours. Her essence was very weak, he realized with a frisson of fear. Almost as if she were unconscious or…

Alarm rippled up his spine, and he headed out of the shop and back toward the house, only to find her lying on the ground a few feet away from the tree where she'd apparently been hanging her clothes to dry.

"Anna!" He knelt beside her, shook her a little, but there was no response. His stomach convulsed as he bent closer to listen to her breath. He was relieved to realize she *was* still breathing, but only once every few seconds. And her heartbeat was weak and erratic.

She was dying. God, no.

He scooped her up into his arms and straightened, then paused as he noticed the words she'd written in the sand after she'd fallen.

I've loved you all my life. And I'm sorry.

It felt as if something inside Diego broke open then, like a dam giving way to the floodwaters it had been holding back. His emotions rolled over him like a tidal wave, and tears blurred his vision. He carried her into the house, laid her on the sofa and then, reluctantly, left her there to check on the strange smell coming from the kitchen.

There was a book in the oven, baking slowly on the center rack. He grabbed a potholder and rescued it, dropping it face-up on the counter. The pages where it had been lying open felt slightly crisp, but for the most part, he thought the book unharmed. Warped by having been soaked in seawater and then oven-dried, but aside from that, it was in surprisingly good shape.

He leaned over it, peering at the handwriting on the pages, knowing it was Anna's. It held her essence. Her energy. Her personality was reflected in the shape of the letters just as it was in the shape of her face.

Later, he told himself. He would look at it later. Right now he had to see about the woman herself. He shut off the oven, then poured a glass of cold water from the pitcher in the fridge. He dampened a clean towel with more of the icy water, then hurried back into the living room, where she lay—so helpless, so fragile—on the sofa.

Leaning closer, he laid the folded dish towel on her forehead, cooling her face, then moved it to cool her neck. As he worked, he spoke to her with his mind, willing her to have the strength to wake, just one last time, before sinking into the sleep from which there was no awakening. Not to this life, at least.

Hear my voice and hold fast to it, Anna. Hear my voice and abide by my will. Gather every bit of strength in you and open your eyes. Talk to me, Anna, just one more time. I command it. Open your eyes. One last time, Anna.

Eventually she stirred, moving her head a little, moaning softly.

"There, that's it. Come on, wake up."

She blinked her eyes open, then stared up at him sleepily. "What happened?"

"You're weaker than either of us realized, Anna."

She nodded slowly, spotting the water and starting to sit up, reaching for it.

"Let me," he said, and he got the glass for her, holding it to her lips and supporting her head.

She drank deeply, then leaned back again and said, "I'm not going to last much longer, am I?"

He thinned his lips, saying nothing.

"I'm dying. You don't have to put up with me for a few weeks, after all. Maybe not even for the rest of tonight."

"Stop it. Stop saying that."

She blinked at his sudden outburst. "Why? It's true. I'm at the end. I can feel it. And then you can toss my body on a pyre and burn me to ash, or haul me out to sea and dump me over the side to feed the fish and be rid of me at last. It's not as if I'll have anything to say in the matter."

"You have everything to say in the matter."

"Do I?"

He nodded. "More than you know. Including…" He bit his lower lip. "Including whether or not to die at all."

His words had clearly reached her. She blinked, hope appearing in her eyes for the first time. "What do you mean, not to die at all?"

He licked his lips, rising from his spot beside the sofa to pace away from her. "I wasn't going to tell you this until…well, until closer to your time. But it seems your time is nearer than we thought."

"How were you planning to tell me anything closer to my time if you sent me away?"

He turned to look back at her. She was watching him, her big blue eyes wider than before, more alert, as if the hope he'd just given her had provided a rush of new strength, as well. "I would have found you. And I would have known when your time was close. I would have felt it, just as I'm feeling it right now."

She blinked rapidly, averting her face and trying to prevent the tears that she could not hope to hide from him. "I'm feeling that, too."

"You know what I am, Anna. You've seen—"

"Yes. You're a vampire." Her eyelids seemed to grow heavy again. They fell slowly closed.

He hurried closer, shook her gently. "Stay with me, Anna. This is important." When she forced her eyes open again, he hurried on. "I'm a vampire, yes. But do you know what that means?"

She shrugged. "You have to drink blood to survive." She was whispering now, leaving long spaces between her words, as if just speaking left her out of breath. "You can't go out in the daylight. And you're…immortal."

"For the most part. We can die. There are ways. We can bleed out. We can go up in a blaze quite easily, either due to the sun or accidental exposure to an open flame. We feel everything intensely. Our senses just grow sharper the longer we live, so that they become extremely acute, from the moment we are changed over, increasing exponentially with each passing year. That means we feel pain more acutely, too. It can debilitate or even kill us. But pleasure…pleasure is…amazing."

She nodded weakly, eyes dropping closed, opening once again. "Why…are you telling me…all this?"

"As a human being, Anna, I had the Belladonna antigen. Just as you do."

Her brows knitted tight as her head tipped sideways. "The same thing that's killing me?"

"Yes. Every vampire had it. It's rare. But it means more than just that you bleed easily and die young. It also means that you can become...what I am. A vampire."

He watched her face, wondering if he would see relief and surprise, or the smug look of triumph he'd chosen to ignore in Cassandra, all those years ago.

But she showed neither of those things. She was still waiting to hear more, as if that was not the revelation that mattered to her. Not at all.

"And then what?" she asked softly.

His brows rose. He was puzzled by both the question and her lack of reaction. "And then you'd be strong, immediately strong, vital, alive. You'd be able to hear every birdsong for a hundred miles, if you wanted. Identify every living thing by its scent from miles away. You could read minds, communicate mentally. You'd run faster than a gazelle, jump higher than anything alive. But you'd never see another sunrise. Never age another day. Never eat another morsel of food, or drink wine or water or anything else. These are heavy prices to pay, Anna."

"I don't imagine I'd be eating or drinking much if I were dead, either," she said very softly. "And all the rest sounds very appealing, Diego, but that's not what I was asking you."

He frowned at her. "Then...what?"

She frowned, staring at him as if she could see inside his mind the way he saw inside hers. "There was another woman, just like me, here with you once, wasn't there? This same situation? I can see it. Who was she?"

"There's no time, Anna," he began.

She swallowed hard. "Then talk fast."

Sighing, he nodded. "Her name was Cassandra. She had the antigen, the syndrome was killing her. She found me here somehow. I think she may have followed me from one of my trips to the mainland. She pretended not to know what I was, what her options were."

"Did you fall in love with her?" Anna asked softly.

"Yes. And she pretended to love me, too, but only until I transformed her. It was all she'd wanted all along, you see. But if she'd simply asked…"

Anna lifted a hand to his cheek and turned him to face her. "You've been shutting me out. Keeping me at arm's length. All because of her. A woman who used you and then threw you away without even knowing what a treasure she had found in you. But I'm not her, Diego. I know how special you are. Somehow, I've always known."

He lifted his brows, hope springing to life in

his heart. "I didn't want to let you get close. I was afraid you would hurt me in the end."

"I won't."

That was all she said. Those two little words. And just like that, what remained of the granite wall he'd erected around his heart shattered into a million glittering bits. He believed her. He actually believed her.

"I don't want to die, Diego," she told him. "I want to live. I never did before, but now...now that I've seen how good life can truly be—now that I've finally figured out how to live—I want to live. But only if I can live here—with you. I think this place...this is paradise. It's all I've ever wanted. *You're* all I've ever wanted, Diego."

He blinked away hot moisture from his eyes and realized it was tears. He hadn't shed tears since Cassandra. This time he shed them in sheer joy.

"I want to share eternity with you, Diego," she told him. "Tell me that's okay with you."

"It's more than okay. I...I love you, Anna. I realized it out in the workshop. I realized I was trying to prevent something that I had no choice about. It was already too late. I love you."

Her smile was wide, and so bright it was contagious. "I love you, too."

"Then…then you're ready?"

"I've been ready for this my entire life," she whispered.

Diego bent closer, pressing his lips to her mouth, kissing her deeply, passionately, and then slowly, he traced a hungry path around her jaw, down over her neck, to her jugular.

She pressed her palms to the back of his head, and closed her eyes as his teeth broke the skin. *"Now,"* she whispered, "I'm in heaven."

* * * * *

IMMORTAL

Maureen Child

Dear Reader,

I love Scotland. Always have. The first time I visited there, it just felt magical to me. Edinburgh castle practically shimmers with the past and the long-dead echoes of those who have loved and died there.

So what better place, I thought, to stage a story about an Immortal Highlander?

Emma Madison is in Edinburgh for the summer on a study program. She never expected to land in the middle of a centuries-long intrigue. And who could possibly have been prepared for Bain Sinclair? He comes to her rescue one dark, scary night—and nothing in Emma's life will ever be the same again.

In this story, you'll find an ancient curse, a heroine with a mind of her own and a hero with a centuries-old code of honor. All set in the shadowy, magical world that is Scotland.

I hope you enjoy spending time with Emma and Bain—I really did.

Happy reading!

Maureen

To Tara Gavin,
the editor who brings so much heart to Nocturne

Chapter 1

"Ye doona hae to go wi' me if ye doona want, though ye hae nowhere else to go nae?"

"Huh?" Two weeks in Edinburgh and Emma Madison still wasn't used to the heavy Scottish accent. Though, in her defense, Cute Blond Guy had a much heavier Scots burr than anyone else she'd encountered since arriving for her summer course at Edinburgh University.

He'd wandered into her study cubicle a half hour before, and since then, they'd been flirting. At least, Emma was pretty sure they were flirting. With that heavy accent, it was sort of hard to tell. But he said his name was Derek, and he was *tall*. Since Emma stood five foot eight, she appreciated a man she had to look up at.

Truth was, though, even if he'd been five foot three, she'd have been grateful for the company. For two hours she'd been sitting in a cramped, generic, study room in the university library all alone, wishing she'd gone to the pub with her dorm mate. But no, she'd done the "right" thing. She'd wanted to somehow prove that her parents were wrong and that spending all this money on a six-week summer session wasn't a waste.

And what did she have to show for being so virtuous? A headache, a growling stomach demanding dinner and a weird sense of… unease. She didn't even want to admit that last bit to herself, but the strange sensation of being watched was hard to ignore.

Just one more reason why she was glad Derek had come to sit with her. Being alone in a practically deserted university library was clearly making her jumpy. No one was watching her. Heck, except for Derek and her, she was pretty sure no one else was there at all. So why, she wondered, couldn't she shake the feeling of impending…something?

She was probably just tired. That and the

fact that the library was too empty. Too quiet. Too...well, creepy.

The building was new and well lit, but beyond the windows, the night was thick and black and almost seemed to be crouched at the glass, waiting for a chance to sneak in and—

"Will ye?"

She frowned, tried to figure out what he'd been saying before and took a shot. "Will I go with you to the pub?"

"Aye, isna tha what I've been sayin'?"

Well, yay her. She'd guessed right. And a trip to a neighborhood pub sounded much better than wading through more nineteenth-century literature at the moment. Naturally, though, her American-honed cautionary instincts kicked in.

Going somewhere with someone she'd never met? Not a good idea. But on the other hand, she'd come to Edinburgh to meet new people, see new things, shake up her life. No point in not seizing the moment when handed the opportunity, right? She was smiling to herself when she happened to glance at Derek and thought she saw...*something*...shift in his eyes. They went from grass green to gray to black and back again to green in the thump of a heartbeat.

Her stomach rolled, but this time fear was in charge, not hunger. She hadn't really seen that, had she? A trick of the light, maybe, she thought as she noted the slight hum of the fluorescent lights overhead. Emma watched him, and the longer she studied him, the less cute Derek became. His smile was fading, his eyes were narrowing and she had the distinct impression he was losing patience with her.

"You'll nae go wi' me, will ye?"

"If that means no way, yeah, that's right," she said, though she wasn't entirely sure why she was suddenly less intrigued by him. There was just something *off*. Something she couldn't put her finger on. Something that warned her to stay exactly where she was.

"Aye, then," he said, his accent sliding into something less comically overdone. "We'll do this here."

"Do what?" Did she really want to know? She slid her chair back, wanting a little more distance between them. Derek had changed so quickly, going from flirtatious to vaguely menacing in a split second. Emma wasn't sure what to do next.

Was there anyone besides the two of them

in this library? Would anyone hear her if she screamed?

Screamed?

Where had that thought come from? Was her mind already sifting through information about Derek and finding things she hadn't really wanted to notice? Was she sensing trouble on a subconscious level?

Oh, she hoped not.

"Look, Derek," she said, standing and gathering up her books and papers, "this has been fun, but I really have to go."

"Not yet." He stood and Emma swallowed hard. Was he going to try to keep her there? Was he some kind of crazed rapist? On drugs or something? That would explain the weird thing with his eyes, but the thought went nowhere in calming Emma down.

"My friends are waiting for me," she said, forcing a smile that felt brittle. That was a big lie. She only knew two people in Edinburgh and they were both at a pub, convinced that Emma would be studying all night.

"They've a long wait, then." His smile faded a bit then as he cocked his head, as if straining to hear sound in the quiet.

She listened, too, hoping to hear a whole

crowd of people approaching the study cubicle. All Emma heard was the hard thump of her own heartbeat.

The steel and glass and chrome library looked innocuous enough—hardly the old-world castlelike building she'd expected to find—but when it was empty, as it was now, it felt sort of…haunted. Of course, Emma had always had a low creep threshold, which was why she never watched horror movies. At sixteen, she'd seen a late-night TV showing of *Friday the 13th,* and hadn't slept for a month.

But that hadn't been real. This was. And she was wasting time. If Derek was hearing someone she wasn't, she'd do well to bring whoever it was closer.

"Hey!" Emma shouted. "In here!"

"Shut yer mouth, woman." Derek's green eyes flashed black, then shifted again until they seemed to roil with flames.

Emma moved back fast, stumbling in her hurry to get away from him, but Derek moved even faster. His feet made no sound, though. It was as if he wasn't really there. And that thought was enough to deepen the chill crawling along Emma's spine.

Then the cold came, settling over the room

like an early frost. Her breath puffed in front of her face and ice cracked and covered the study table like a glistening tablecloth. Derek stood in front of her, his lips peeled back from his teeth in a parody of a smile, and the temperature in the room plummeted even further.

Fear spiked inside Emma, slicing at her insides, making her breath hitch and her pulse race. Her mouth was dry, her throat was tight. There was nowhere to run. The cubicle was small, enclosed, with one way out, and Derek was blocking that path.

To escape, she'd have to go through him, and for the first time in her life, Emma was grateful that she wasn't exactly a delicate flower of a girl. She was an athlete and not exactly anorexic. In fact, her best friend had once said that Emma had enough boobs to build two healthy women.

Right now, though, she'd trade the boobs for a baseball bat. Or an Uzi.

She swallowed her fear and the wild racings of her mind. Why was it so cold? What was happening? Who was he? He couldn't simply be some run-of-the-mill lunatic. There was more going on here, much more, but she had no idea what it was. Or how to combat it or even if she'd live through the next ten seconds.

So the only choice she had was to play dumb. The innocent. To try to ease Derek back into the mildly flirtatious mood he'd been in only moments ago.

"Look," she said, shivering as the temperature continued to drop and her mind screamed silently. "You seem like a nice guy and everything…" Soothe the crazy person, she told herself. Keep your voice even, soft. Don't be threatening, and for heaven's sake don't ask him why his eyes change colors or how he's making the room so damn cold your hands are turning blue. And most importantly, if he rushes you, remember that you played soccer for five years and you've got a hell of a kick.

Good to know that one corner of her mind was still working even while another corner was curled up in a ball keening.

"You're a Campbell, are you not?"

"Huh?" Okay, she hadn't been expecting *that*. What did her mother's maiden name have to do with anything and how had this guy known about it, anyway?

She backed up again, keeping one trembling, nearly frostbitten hand stretched out behind her, hoping to not trip and fall like a dumb heroine in a horror movie.

"You are." Derek sidled closer again, still moving without sound, and now Emma realized he'd done that from the beginning. She hadn't heard him enter her study cubicle. It was more like she'd looked up and there he was. Why hadn't she noticed that before?

Why was she only now seeing that nothing about him was normal? He smiled as if he could guess what she was thinking and now his eyes were black again. Black and empty. "You're a Campbell. I can smell it on you. Your blood sings to me."

Her *blood?* Not only crazy, but a wannabe vampire? Oh, crap. Emma was in deep trouble.

"Give me what I need."

"Therapy?"

Then he was on her. So fast she hadn't even seen him move. So fast she hadn't had a chance to kick him or even to draw in an icy breath to scream. In a blur of soundless speed, he closed the distance between them and grabbed her so hard she dropped her books, and the papers tucked inside swirled in the cold air like overblown snowflakes.

"Step away from the woman, demon."

A deep voice, dark and rich and full of threat, rolled out around them like a clap of thunder.

Emma didn't feel the reprieve that voice should have provided, though, because Derek's hands on her arms tightened, his fingernails digging through her long-sleeved yellow T-shirt to slice into her skin. She felt blood trickling down her arms, glanced down to see it seeping through her shirt. She felt sick to her stomach.

"Guardian," Derek whispered, his once-pronounced accent now completely gone, and his voice a raw scrape on the air. "Move and she dies."

"Don't move!" Emma shouted, looking past Derek to the man standing in the open doorway. The instant she saw *him,* she knew instinctively that nothing would ever be the same again.

At least six foot five, *he* had shoulder-length black hair and pale blue eyes. His jaw was square and his nose looked as if it had been broken and reset a few times. His shoulders seemed as broad as a football field and the long, black leather coat he wore over black jeans and a white shirt was just the camouflage he needed to hide the sword he carried.

The sword?

Oh, God. What was going on?

And in that one horrible moment, she realized that she'd spent a lot of time lately wishing for some excitement in her life. This reminded her of her mother's all-time favorite saying.

Be careful what you wish for.

"You don't belong here," the sword-wielding giant announced, his deep voice nearly rattling the windowpanes.

"Excuse me?" Emma said, outraged despite the fact that Derek's fingers dug even harder into her upper arms.

"I wasn't talking to you," the huge man in the doorway said, those pale blue eyes fixing on the guy with a death grip on Emma.

"Oh. Okay." Well, good, she thought, one half of her mind still worried about that sword, while the other half was happy to have him on her side. Then she turned her face to her captor. "Look, just let me go and we all walk away."

"No, we don't." The man in the doorway looked more formidable than ever as those icy eyes of his fixed on his prey.

"Not helping," Emma told him, struggling wildly to pull free of Derek's grip.

"I'll not let her go," the blond said, and instead of releasing her, he wrapped one arm around her throat and pulled her back tight against him. "She's mine now."

"Yours?" Emma dragged her short, neat nails

across Derek's skin, but he acted as though he didn't feel it. She had to escape. Had to get out. How had a study night at the library turned into a scene from one of those movies she hated? How had she, Emma Madison, landed in the middle of some weird hostage situation?

Chapter 2

"You can't win this and you know it, demon." Bain Sinclair stared at the demon he'd tracked through most of Edinburgh and couldn't help the mild sense of disappointment he felt. This miserable creature would prove no test of his strength. Would offer no real battle. Were there no strong demons left to fight in this infernal city? Was this the best demon the worlds had to show him?

Still, as an immortal Guardian, it was Sinclair's duty to capture the damned demon and send it back through a portal to the hell dimension it had escaped. As there were thousands of different demons, so, too, were there many different dimensions. All of them crowding up against this world, all of them housing demons hoping to claim the earth and subjugate humanity.

The Guardians were all that stood between the demon worlds and this one. Sinclair, like his fellow Guardians, had taken an oath centuries ago to protect the human world from those that would destroy it. Even if it were only this puny demon with delusions of grandeur.

"I'll kill her."

Sinclair scowled at the creature who held the woman so tightly. He didn't dare take his eyes off his prey long enough to inspect the hostage. Even small, inferior demons could prove challenging at times, and he'd no wish to see the human woman harmed.

"Get him off of me!" The woman's voice was loud and demanding.

Then Sinclair did spare her a quick look and felt a hard jolt to his system. She was tall, with eyes as green as the highland hills and short, red hair with curls that looked as soft as eiderdown. Her mouth was full and lush, her chin stubborn and her body the stuff dreams were made of. Her curves were as lush as her mouth and desire pulsed inside him with a heat he'd never known before.

Who was she? Who was this woman who inflamed both him *and* a demon? A question that must be answered. But first… Lifting the sword he'd carried for nearly a thousand years, Sinclair moved within a foot of his prey in the blink of an eye.

"I swear I'll kill her," the creature spat at him, his eyes wheeling as he desperately searched for an escape that wouldn't be found.

Pale blue eyes locked on the demon, his features schooled into a calm mask of determination, Sinclair shook his head. "You won't, you wee weasel of a demon. You need her. As you've said yourself."

"There are other Campbells," the demon said slyly.

"Campbell?" Sinclair stopped short, glared first at the demon, then at the woman and then back again. "She's a Campbell?"

Before anything more was said, the woman clearly became tired of waiting to be released. Lifting her foot, she dug the heel of her boot into the top of the demon's foot. The creature let loose a shout of pain, released her and she instantly dropped to the floor. Scrabbling backward on her butt, she moved as quickly as she could, while keeping an eye on the men closing in on each other.

Sinclair took advantage of her courage. Moving quickly, he tossed the tip of his sword high and allowed the Guardian netting, a fine mesh of magically warded silver he'd attached to the blade, to drape across the demon, who was trying to run. Instantly, the creature was trapped, and the more it struggled, the tighter it was held. Only when he was sure his prey was incapacitated, did Sinclair allow himself to turn and face the woman.

"Who are you?" he demanded. "And why are you with a demon?"

"I'm not *with* him—" She broke off and sent a look at the creature trapped within the netting, rolling about on the floor and cursing in an unintelligible language. "A *demon?*"

"Aye."

"You'll pay, Guardian," Derek suddenly screamed in unaccented English.

"Aye," Sinclair muttered, "so your kind always say." Then he focused on the woman, now gathering up her things from the floor and pushing herself to her feet. "Tell me, then. Who are you and why did the demon want you?"

"My name's Emma Madison and who are you?"

"Bain Sinclair. Guardian to this post and the one who's asking the questions, lass."

"I'm not a lass," she argued. "And what's a guardian and you know what? Never mind. I don't want to know what's going on here, who you are, who he is, how you threw that net or any other damn thing. I just want out of here."

She backed away and Sinclair's eyes narrowed on her. She wouldn't be leaving until he knew what was happening. The fact that she was a Campbell didn't set well with him, since Sinclair had died during a skirmish with the treacherous clan centuries ago. But he was willing to overlook that for now, especially since she had a spine. Unless he discovered that, true to her bloodline, this lass was somehow conspiring with the demon world to unleash hell on Earth.

"I'm just going to leave now and you two can—" Her voice faded away as her gaze locked with his, and Sinclair felt her fear spike even as he watched it register on her features.

Guardians were telepaths, able to read the minds of those they wished. Normally, Sinclair turned that power down, not wanting to be assailed by the thoughts of others. But in this instance, he needed to know what the woman knew. Needed to have more information. And in a rush, her wildly disorganized thoughts streamed into Sinclair's mind.

You're both crazy, her mind screamed. *I don't know what you want. Or what he wanted, but right now, all I want is to get back to my dorm room, close the door and barricade it. Maybe this is a dream,* she thought frantically, helplessly, *maybe I'll wake up in my room and realize I'm just jet-lagged or hungover or something and none of this is real and—*

"'Tis real," Sinclair said brusquely, interrupting the wild flow of her thoughts.

"What?" She blinked up at him. "How did you know— What *are* you?"

"Time enough for that discussion later, Emma Madison," he said, turning his gaze back to the trapped demon. "First I must return this one to his hell."

"Hell? Oh, God…"

Sinclair bent down, lifted the demon as if he weighed nothing at all, then slung him, still netted, over his shoulder. "Come. We'll talk, you and I. I've need of answers and you're the one who has them, I'm thinking."

"Hold it," she said, shaking her head, shifting

her gaze between him and Derek. "I'm not going anywhere with you."

"Aye. You are. Either walking or across my shoulder. Your choice."

"I'll scream."

Sinclair waved one hand through the air, effectively sealing the three of them in a bubble of privacy. Wrapped in this field of energy, Guardians could move unseen through crowds of humans. And trapped as she was now, with him, the woman could scream her blasted head off and none would be aware of her.

"Go ahead, then," he said, already walking, expecting her to follow, for where else would she go now that he'd trapped her as neatly as he had the demon. "But once you've seen it'll do no good, I'd take it as a kindness if you'd shut the bleeding hell up."

Insulted, enraged and just plain terrified, Emma was dragged in his wake as if tied to him by an invisible tether. She had to run to keep up with his long-legged stride and she noticed as they moved through the library that the building was indeed deserted. Long hallways lit by the flickering overhead lights seemed to stretch on forever. Empty rooms stood sentinel as she passed and Emma's heartbeat quickened. If Sinclair hadn't come to her rescue, God knew what Derek might have done to her.

And he'd been right. Screaming wouldn't do her a bit of good. There was no one to hear her.

The big man stopped suddenly and she collided with his back. It was like walking into a brick wall. He didn't budge. Didn't rock unsteadily on his feet. He was a mountain. The proverbial hard place. And now she was trapped between him and a…demon?

Her gaze fixed on Derek, she stepped back and slammed into an invisible wall behind her, then shot another look at Bain Sinclair. Was he safety or a new threat?

The man Derek had called guardian turned his pale, icy blue eyes on her. Slowly, he raked his gaze up and down her body until she felt as though her skin was on fire. Tiny electrical jolts shot through her system under his steady regard. She took another breath, fought down that sizzle of whatever it was and focused on the most important point at the moment.

She was alone with not one but *two* crazies.

Instantly, Emma pictured the headlines on her hometown newspaper in California: "College

Student Killed by Sword-wielding Psycho in Scotland."

Not what she'd been hoping for when she signed up for this summer course. But then she'd never expected to run into a man like this one, either. Who would?

"A new portal's been opened here," Sinclair said, lifting his sword high.

"I don't see anything," Emma muttered, not sure if she should tell the truth or placate the crazy man.

"You will." Then Sinclair began speaking, his deep rumble of a voice rolling out around her like black velvet. Words in a language that sounded as old as time and just as mysterious filled the air and Emma held her breath, half-afraid to face what might happen next.

Then she saw it. A wash of pale yellow light that streamed into the room as it brightened, elongated, becoming what looked like a window into another world. As Sinclair's voice rolled on, images formed and faded within that window. Colors, shapes, creatures, flickered on and off like a slide show of kaleidoscopic breadth. So many things, too many. And none of it made sense.

"Hold!" Sinclair's shout brought the flickering images to a standstill.

Emma looked into the window of light and saw beyond to a landscape that was so foreign she could hardly take it in. Black trees, twisted into shapes both horrifying and intriguing. Skeletal creatures slipping in and out of the shadows. Twin bloodred suns shining from a black sky, and a hot wind, heavy with the scent of spices, raced through the opening into Emma's world.

"What is that?" She shook her head, looked at Sinclair as he swung Derek down off his back and quickly freed him from the netting.

"There are many hells," Sinclair muttered, keeping a tight grip on the back of Derek's neck. "And even more demons. This one belongs in that hell," he said, jerking his head at the weirdly pulsing window of light.

Derek stared at her, licked his lips with a tongue that was as red as the weird suns staining that foreign sky and then he whispered, "He can't save you from me, you know. I've got the flavor of you now." He lifted his fingers, still damp with her blood, tasted them and sighed. "I'll find you. When he's nowhere near. I'll find you."

"Leave off, demon, and go back to your hell," Sinclair ordered, and gave Derek a shove that sent him tumbling through the window of light and fire.

When he was gone, the portal snapped shut and disappeared as if it had never been. All that remained was the faint scent of spice and the huge man at Emma's side.

"Oh, my God." Her brain was spinning. This was like being drunk without the good time. Nothing of what she'd experienced could possibly be real. So the only explanation was she'd had a stroke or something. Maybe she was even now lying in a dream-filled coma in an Edinburgh hospital. Heck, maybe she was still at home, dreaming about going to Scotland. And if that were true, she wouldn't be anywhere near the country she'd dreamed of visiting all her life.

But beneath her, the floor felt cold and hard and the sultry scent of spices still hung in the air. So no, she wasn't dreaming. This was all real. Impossibly, incredibly, *real.* "What is happening to me?"

"A long story, lass. One better told in safer places." The giant of a man held out one hand to her and Emma wanted to take it. She just wasn't sure she'd be able to stand even with his help.

She needn't have worried.

"I might've known it would be a Campbell

to bring me more grief." He shook his head, his long black hair settling behind his back as he grabbed hold of her, pulled her to her feet and, in one easy movement, tossed her across his shoulder—exactly as he had with the demon only a few moments ago. Emma pushed herself up against his back, but she'd no hope of freeing herself, anyway. He was even stronger than he looked.

Locking one arm across her knees, Sinclair muttered something about damned women and blasted Campbells as he stalked from the library and into the cold, clear night.

Chapter 3

Emma's kidnapper/hero lived in luxury.

His palatial estate took up half a city block not far from Princes Street, and outside the floor-to-ceiling windows, the lights of Edinburgh twinkled like fallen stars. Inside the house, she stood in a book-filled study, with a fire blazing in a man-size hearth. Leather chairs dotted the floor as if silently inviting guests to get comfortable.

She was so far from comfy, Emma thought she might never relax again.

Her gaze slid to the man standing with his back to the fire. His coat and sword were gone and still he was formidable. Broad chest,

muscular legs and thickly muscled arms—the
man was a walking weapon. She should be
terrified of him—and yet, there was something
inside her that…yearned. That ached for him.
Wanted to crawl inside his embrace and stay
there. Ridiculous, she told herself. She was
clearly having some sort of delayed reaction to
what had happened to her.

"Think, Emma. What would a Cirico demon
want with a Campbell?"

"I don't know," she said for at least the fifth
time since he'd brought her here to this…palace.
For the past hour, he'd questioned her, made
her repeat her conversation with Derek and
in general hadn't given her a moment's peace.
"Until an hour ago, I didn't even know there *were*
demons."

"Yet he found you. Marked you." Bain nodded
at her neatly bandaged arms.

For a second or two, she remembered him
carefully rolling her long-sleeved shirt up and
tenderly bandaging the slices Derek's fingernails
had made on her skin. In those moments, Sinclair
had seemed gentle. But it hadn't lasted long.

"What does that mean exactly?" she asked.
"He 'marked me.'"

"He's tasted your blood—"

"Don't remind me—"

"When he escapes again—"

"When?"

Bain nodded. "The blasted demons never stay gone for long. And once he's out, he will find you."

"Oh, God." Her knees folded and she sat down right where she was, landing on an ornate rug that was more beautiful than padded. "What can I do?"

"You will stay here. With me."

A decree, she thought, said with the same tone of authority that an ancient lord of the manor would have used to an annoying peasant. She wanted to be insulted, but, really, she was grateful. And what did that say? She didn't know this guy from a hole in the wall. For all she knew, he could be just as crazy as that...*demon.* But no. Her mind argued with her even as she considered it. He wasn't crazy. He was the hero in this picture. He'd saved her from whatever Derek had had planned. And he'd brought her here and bandaged her—she remembered the soft touch of his hands on her skin and recalled, very clearly, the buzz of sensation just being near him had caused.

So yes, she was grateful to him and intrigued

by him and, God knows, she didn't want to think about facing Derek alone—still, she couldn't just stay here with Bain Sinclair indefinitely.

"For how long?" she asked.

Those wide shoulders moved in a lazy shrug as if her question were of no consequence. "For however long it takes."

She shook her head, despite the tremors racking her body. "I can't do that. I have classes. Obligations."

"You will stay."

Emma lifted her chin and narrowed her eyes. She never had been one to follow orders easily. Even when it was the logical, rational thing to do. "You can't make me."

Bain smiled at her as he walked stealthily across the room. "I can and I will. Where would you go for help if not to me? The police? They'd think you crazy. Lock you away and then the demon would have you."

"Damn it." He was right. But that wasn't her only option. She could catch a plane and—

"Would you think to run to your home in America? Would you lead the demon to your family?"

She glared at him. "How are you doing that? Reading my mind?"

"For you, Emma Campbell," he said, not bothering to answer the question, "there is no one but me."

"Madison," she corrected absently, hating to admit that he was right. She couldn't very well take a plane to California, leading Derek right to her family's door. "My name is Madison. My mother was a Campbell before she married."

He sneered and in that movement she saw him as he should have been. Standing on a Highland mountain, hair blowing in a cold wind, bare, muscular legs braced wide apart, a kilt flapping at his knees and his plaid tossed over one shoulder. The image in her mind was so real, so detailed, it was more like a memory than imagination.

Oh, Emma had read plenty of books with Highland heroes, and Bain Sinclair was the personification of every one of them. Arrogant. Proud. Determined. Funny that she'd never before realized how annoying those traits would be in real life.

"The Campbells have been known for treachery since time began," he said, sneer still in place. "Diluting that blood through marriage does not change it. I knew many of your clan in the Highlands where I grew up, and learned early never to trust one of them. Tell me, then, why I should trust you."

"Nobody asked you to trust me," she reminded him. "You're the one who carried me out of the university library and brought me here. You're the one who's insisting I stay. I don't even know you. Why should I trust *you?*"

His lip curled, defining that sneer of his even further. "As I'm the one who saved your pretty backside from a hungering demon, I'm thinking I've earned the right to demand the trust of a Campbell. Yet, I warn you. If there's a Campbell involved in demon treachery," he went on as if she hadn't spoken, "I'll discover the truth of it. You can no more hide the truth of it than you can hide the blood that runs in your veins."

Emma refused to have this conversation sitting at his feet and looking up at him. She stood, stabbed her index finger at him and said, "My mother is a Campbell and is one of the nicest human beings on the *planet.* Don't you talk about her like that. And while we're at it, I'm the one who should be worried about trusting *you.*"

"I'll remind you yet again that I saved your beautiful hide, didn't I?"

Beautiful? Not to mention *pretty backside?* She shook her head. *Concentrate, Emma.*

"I could have handled him myself," she argued. "Eventually."

He laughed and the sound nearly rattled the windowpanes. "Lie to yourself all you want, woman. But don't expect me to believe it. You were a tasty morsel to the demon and well you know it. If not for me—"

"Which begs the question," Emma interrupted, "what were you doing there, anyway? How come you were so handy to the scene? For all I know you were working with Derek the Troll."

"You accuse me of being in league with a demon?" He looked astonished at the idea.

"How do I know?" She waved one hand at him. "You're the one carrying a sword for God's sake. You're the one who kidnapped *me*. I didn't ask for any of this. And besides, we know I wasn't working with that thing. It almost killed me, remember?"

"He could have, but didn't," Sinclair told her, studying her carefully as if looking for some sign that she was what she claimed to be. She saw wary suspicion in his eyes and Emma stiffened. "He wanted something from you."

"Well, I don't know what. What could a demon want with me, anyway? I'm a student, for pity's sake," she muttered, then narrowed her eyes on him. "And I'm pretty darn disappointed in Scotland, let me tell you. I've dreamed about coming here all my life and never once did I dream about *demons*. I thought this was going to be a fun trip to a gorgeous place and all of a sudden it's a nightmare."

"Edinburgh is not all of Scotland," he said, dismissing the ancient city with another of his sneers. "'Tis a city like any other, with too many people and too many cars and too much noise for a man to think. There's good and bad here, like any other city of its kind. If you want beauty, you must go to my true home. The Highlands."

For one brief moment, her heart fluttered. It was the way he said the word *Highlands*. Like a man missing a lover. She heard his affection for the place in his tone and knew that this at least was one thing they shared. Emma had been reading about and dreaming of the Highlands of Scotland for as long as she could remember. But she only said, "You're no Highlander. You don't talk like one."

He frowned at her. "How am I supposed to speak, then, lass?"

"You know—" she waved one hand at him "—doona, dinna, canna, willna…"

He stared at her for a long minute and the

flames crackling in the hearth were the only sound in the room beyond the pounding of her own heart. Then he laughed again. He threw his head back, planted both fists on his hips and laughed loud and long, the booming music of his laughter echoing off the walls, the ceiling and settling down over her like a warm blanket.

Despite her anger, Emma felt something inside her stir in response. Her blood heated, every nerve jangled in anticipation. There was something old within her. Something ancient. Something that recognized this man. She felt as though she'd been waiting for him. She didn't understand, but as she watched him every cell in her body leaped to life as they never had before. She *knew* Bain Sinclair with a bone-deep knowledge that had no explanation.

She'd never experienced anything like this before. Emma's earlier worries about being with him disappeared as she realized that through the fear and the worry and the confusion one thing rang clear in her mind. This man was where she belonged. This man was sanctuary.

This man was *everything*.

When his laughter finally died away, he looked down at her, still grinning, and Emma's heart stuttered painfully in her chest.

"That's foolishness, lass," he said, looking directly into her eyes. His gaze was steady and so pale a blue Emma felt as though she were looking at pieces of the sky.

"No Highlander talks like that. At least, not anymore." His smile faded as he led her to a nearby sofa, sat her down and then seated himself beside her. "Centuries ago, perhaps." He looked toward the window, but his gaze was fixed on something much farther away than the night outside. "Many things were different then. We walked our land as kings and fought and held it against countless enemies. But times change and a wise man changes with them."

"We? Centuries?" Her voice was a whisper. Her gaze locked on his profile as he seemed to stare into a past she could never fully understand. Was he really saying what she thought he was saying?

She swallowed hard. He spoke as if he'd seen those changes come and roll past. Had personally ridden the tide of history. It didn't make sense, but then what about tonight's happenings did? Why shouldn't she be sitting in a veritable palace in Edinburgh with a Highlander who was as mystical and mysterious as the feelings he engendered inside her?

He turned his face to hers, looked deeply into her eyes and said only, "Aye, lass. Centuries."

She met his gaze and saw the truth shining there at her. Of course he was centuries old. Of course he was part of the magic of Scotland. Breath caught in her lungs, she whispered, "How many?"

"Several."

Her stomach did a quick pitch and roll before cautiously settling again. It seemed impossible, of course. No one lived forever. But what about that night so far *had* been possible? Emma gave herself a mental pat on the back for accepting this latest piece of craziness so easily. Was her brain just giving up the fight for logic? No, she thought, with another good look at Bain Sinclair. It wasn't hard to believe in what he was saying because he was exactly the kind of man legends were built around.

He met her gaze squarely, silently, as if giving her time to adjust. But in a very weird way, knowing that he was centuries old made perfect sense. He was simply too *male* to be a modern-day man.

"You're telling me you've lived hundreds of years." Her gaze moved over his features, cataloging them carefully, etching the harsh planes and angles into her memory. Unnecessary, though, she thought, since a part of her recognized him. Knew him. He looked no more than thirty-five, yet his eyes were as ancient as time itself. "How is that possible?"

"I'm an immortal."

"Immortal." His features were calm, almost dispassionate, and she knew instinctively he wasn't lying. She took a deep breath, blew it out and dragged in another one. "Oh, God."

"I'll not hurt you, Emma," he said, then frowned slightly, "unless I find you're in league with that demon, after all."

"I'm not, but you…" She pushed both hands through her short, red hair and rubbed at her scalp as if she could somehow slow down her racing thoughts with a quick massage. "How—when—why?"

Still keeping his gaze locked on hers, he said softly, "I died in 1046 and was made an immortal Guardian. We few protect this world from the demons trying to destroy it."

"Immortals. Demons," she whispered, caught in the heat of those amazing eyes of his. "Guardians, for Pete's sake. One of us is really crazy, Bain. And I don't think it's you. So what does that say about me?"

"That you're a woman with a cool head on her shoulders," he told her, one corner of his mouth tipping up. "One not willing to take things at surface truth. A woman who trusts her instincts."

"Right." She blew out a breath, scrubbed her hands up and down her forearms and felt the bandages he'd applied as soon as he'd brought her here. He'd saved her from Derek. Treated her cuts. Fed her. Was offering her protection. And now, he'd trusted her with a secret she knew instinctively he didn't share with many others. She was being pulled into a world she never would have thought existed and somehow…it felt *right*.

"I don't understand any of this," she whispered. Emma looked at him and knew that everything he was saying was the absolute truth. But her heart was at war with her brain, that still screamed for logic.

Flames snapped and hissed in the hearth; somewhere in the house a grandfather clock bonged out the hour, and outside in the city the world rolled on. While Emma listened, Bain talked. He told her everything. Told her about life in the eleventh century. How he'd died at the hands of a Campbell who'd sold out their cause

against the British for a handful of gold coins
and a new castle.

She saw it all; the past was alive and vivid, as
if she, too, had lived in the world he described.
As if a part of her had always been with him.

Then he told her that at the moment of his
death he'd met a being called Michael and was
given a choice. His soul could continue on
to whatever awaited it, or he could live as an
immortal and battle evil through the centuries.
Bain had accepted the challenge and made a
home in the Highlands where he'd lived off and
on for hundreds of years. This house, where
they stayed in Edinburgh, belonged to another
Guardian, Karras, who was off now on business
of his own.

That was the only reason Bain was in the city.
He was watching over the portals until Karras
returned. Then Bain would go back to his home
in the Highlands.

By the time he finished speaking, Emma's
head was spinning. She heard every word,
watched his face, the shifting emotions flashing
across his features as he told her of the passage
of time. How he'd lived, alone, in a castle near
his ancestral clan.

The Highlanders there didn't ask questions of

a man. Didn't wonder why he never aged. The people there still believed in magic and the world of the Fae. They understood that not all of life was simple black and white and that there were no answers to some questions—so they didn't ask them.

"And you live alone," she said, feeling a tear in her heart at the thought of him existing in solitude for eons. Everything in her wanted to reach out to him. To somehow ease the loneliness that must be clawing at him. Surprised by the strength of her reaction to him, Emma tried to rein in her own feelings as he answered her question.

"Yes, I live alone. I've never felt a hunger to change that." He turned his head again, to look at her now. "Until you."

"Me?" Her heart shivered, but still she shook her head. "You don't even like me. I'm a Campbell, remember?"

"Not something I'm going to forget, lass. But the heart of it is, you call to me and I know you feel the same."

"I do, yes," she said, scooting back on the couch as he shifted to lean toward her. "But it doesn't make sense, Bain. We just met." Love at first sight only happened in the movies, she thought. Or in books. It wasn't real life, and even if it was, it wouldn't happen to *her*. "I don't know what I feel," she hedged, her heartbeat quickening as he reached for her hand.

The instant his fingers touched hers, the moment his palm slid against hers, heat slammed through her. It was so much more than desire, though. This felt like her entire body was awakening all at once. As if she hadn't even really been *alive* until this moment. There was something inevitable about it. As if she'd been made for him. As if her body had only been waiting for him to show up so it could welcome him.

How could she fight something so elemental?

"Do you feel that?" he asked, his deep voice a raw hush of sound. "The fire between us? The flash of lightning?"

Instantly, heat spilled from him, slid into her and sped through her veins like flames dancing atop a river of gasoline. She burned. She ached. She felt a connection to him she'd never known before. And when she looked into his eyes again, she knew he felt it, too. What was the point in denying it? "I do. What is it? What does it mean?"

"If it means what I think it does, you'll not be leaving me. Ever."

"Hold on here, Bain," she said, needing to put the brakes on, for her own sanity's sake if not for anything else. "There's no way I can just stay here forever. I hardly know you. I have a life. Parents. A brother and—"

He kissed her.

Emma's brain shut down and her body took over. Its needs supplanted everything else. Words died. Thoughts splintered. The touch of his mouth on hers dissolved everything but the very sensations it created. One corner of Emma's mind fought to hide what she was feeling, but Bain wouldn't allow that. He gave her more, demanded more. His mouth, his tongue, his breath, all worked together to drown her in more soul-shaking sensations than she'd ever known before.

Wrapping his hard, muscular arms around her, he leaned back on the sofa and drew her with him until she was wrapped across the top of him. She felt every square inch of his huge, amazing body and that only fed the flames already licking at her insides. His hands slid down her back to her behind and pressed her to him until she felt the rock-hard length of him and she knew exactly how much he wanted her.

She groaned as his tongue tangled with hers. Sighed as he lifted his hips into hers and she wiggled atop him as if trying desperately to get even closer to him. That tiny, logical voice in the back of her mind shrieked even louder, demanding that Emma stop. Think.

But she wasn't the one who called a halt to what was the most sensuous experience of her life.

Bain pulled back from her, breaking the kiss even as warning bells sounded in his mind. There was more here than simple lust. More even than the slender threads of connection he'd felt ever since first laying eyes on the woman. This was deeper, richer, unlike anything he'd ever experienced with any of the countless women he'd been with during the centuries of his life.

His heart thundering in his chest, Bain sat up, gently easing Emma off his chest and away from the aching erection that was demanding he get closer to her, not farther away. But he'd be damned if he allowed his cock to be making his decisions for him at his age.

It wasn't just lust pounding through him, Bain

told himself as he fought to keep from reaching for her again. His gaze locked on her, he noted her swollen lips, her disarranged clothing and her quick, uneven breath.

He groaned inwardly as he silently admitted that he'd been right in his suspicions about the attraction he felt for Emma. From the very first moment he'd set eyes on her, he'd felt it. The *bond* that had leaped to life the moment she was near him. Now, Guardian legends raced through his brain—tales of Destined Mates. The one woman meant to be with a certain Guardian. How his body would know hers. His soul would recognize hers. How their connection would strengthen a Guardian's powers even while tying him more closely to the human world he protected.

Bain had to acknowledge that he hadn't put much faith in the legends. After all, a man living centuries alone could make himself insane, waiting and searching for a Mate that would never appear. Instead, Bain had put the legends from his mind and focused his energies and his great strength on the task given to him. Fighting demons.

Now his world had changed in the fast blink of an eye. She was here. In front of him. A woman from modern times that called to the ancient warrior within him. Was Emma the one? Was this woman his promised Mate?

There was only one real way to know for sure. According to legend, only his Destined Mate would be able to hear a Guardian's thoughts. He looked into her eyes and sent her a mental command.

Take off your clothes.

She laughed shortly and straightened her shirt before pushing one hand through her tousled hair. "In your dreams."

Bleeding, buggering hell.

The Fates were ever trifling with a man. But this was too much. To send him a Destined Mate after centuries of solitary life would seem a gift to some. But the fact that she was a Campbell proved that those very Fates had a most perverse sense of humor.

"Do you realize, lass," he said on a sigh, "that I didn't say that out loud?"

A moment passed, then two. And finally, her eyes widened, her mouth dropped open and she stared up at him. "But I heard—"

"Aye, you heard my thoughts. And that can only mean one thing. You're mine, lass."

Chapter 4

She was his.

Three days later, Bain's words were still circling in Emma's mind and she was no closer to being able to accept them. How could she? How was she supposed to believe that she was Bain's Destined Mate? The one woman in the world meant to be with him?

"Not that you'd know it from the way he's treating me," she muttered to no one. Three days she'd been locked away in the Edinburgh mansion with the one man in the world who was supposed to be destined for her and had he made one solitary move since that amazing kiss?

No, he hadn't.

She wasn't disappointed, though. It wasn't as if she *wanted* to jump into bed with a virtual stranger—well, okay, maybe she did. But if he was right, then he wasn't really a stranger, either, was he?

And if she *was* this legendary Destined Mate, how could it possibly work out for them? He was an immortal. She wasn't. So was she supposed to stay with him until she was old and wrinkly and then what? He moves on, looking for another "mate" while she checks into the Old Mates' Home?

She sighed a little and walked into the garden of Bain's elegant mansion. Beyond the gray brick wall surrounding the back garden lay Edinburgh, the city she'd dreamed of visiting. The city she'd always felt drawn to. Now she had to wonder if her longing for Scotland had been her own subconscious trying to get her close to Bain. Was it possible that she once had been a woman in love with Bain, and was now reborn to get another shot at a happily ever after?

"God. It sounds like a bad plot in a sappy movie." But what other explanation was there? How did she know so much about him? How had she seen glimpses of his life? How had she read his thoughts? Why did she feel a "bond" with him?

Had she somehow known that coming here, to Scotland, would give her the opportunity to find the one man in the world she belonged with? And if so, *why?* To torture herself? Even if she was his Destined Mate, nothing could come of it. He was immortal and she was mortal. And that was just the beginning of their problems.

She was also an American with a family back home waiting for her. She couldn't just settle down with a Scotsman they'd never even met! And what was she supposed to do about school? She hadn't finished her degree yet and no way was she going to stop before she had.

Already because of this bizarre situation, she'd missed a couple of classes she couldn't afford to skip. But every time she thought about going back to the university, she pictured Derek the Troll showing up and trying to drink her blood or something even more disgusting.

Emma sighed, tried to push those thoughts out of her mind and focused instead on everything that had been happening lately. She'd called her parents to check in, not that she could mention anything about the weirdness of her life at the moment. What was she supposed to say about that, anyway? *Mom, Dad, I've met an immortal and we're supposed to be together forever.* Oh, yeah, that'd go over well. They'd have her on the first plane home, and from there to a lovely rubber room.

It wasn't easy talking to people you loved and lying to them. She felt terrible about it, but she honestly couldn't think of a way around the situation, either. Then, after calling home, she'd contacted the university to let them know that she would be missing a few classes. God knew how many, of course, but that was something she didn't want to think about yet.

Just as she didn't want to think about the whole Destined Mate thing.

The way Bain had explained it to her, once Mates made love, they were each of them strengthened. His powers as a Guardian would be enhanced and whatever innate strengths she possessed would also be made stronger. There would be a physical and mental connection between them. She could already hear his thoughts as he could hers—which was uncomfortable, but if they were to have sex, that psychic bond would become stronger, too.

That was probably why he was making such a concerted effort to avoid her. She already felt more connected to him than she ever had to anyone else in her life. She couldn't sleep at night without dreaming about him. She woke up every morning aching for his touch.

Scrubbing her hands up and down her arms to dispel the chill racing along her skin, she wondered how she would ever be able to live without Bain if they ever did make love. Wouldn't she miss him for the rest of her life? Wouldn't she ache for him and pine for him and in general lead a long, miserable life all alone? And when she died a, hopefully, old woman, he would still be as he was today. Young. Strong.

Gorgeous.

And alone, she added, letting her gaze sweep across the tidy gardens and neatly clipped hedges. She knew Bain wouldn't be able to find another Mate. She was it for him. So when she died, he would be left to just keep going and going, continuing on through eternity, so alone. So solitary. So separate from the very world he fought so hard to defend.

Her heart ached for him, as if she were already feeling the pain that he would be forced to live with. But nowhere in his description of the Mate thing had he said anything about *love*. So what did that really make her? Bain's own personal battery charger? Not only would he get sex, but he'd become stronger. Was that why he wanted her here? Was it really not about protecting her, but strengthening Bain? And how would she ever know for sure?

"How'm I supposed to deal with this?" she wondered aloud, tipping her head back to stare up at the heavy gray clouds.

"You think it's easy for me, then?"

Emma whirled around and watched as Bain stepped out of the house and walked with long strides across the patio. He wore his black jeans, a black shirt, and as his long black coat flapped around his knees, she caught glimpses of the sword still strapped to his side. She knew instinctively that he'd been out in the city, demon hunting.

And how weird was it that she was getting used to that phrase?

A cold, damp wind lifted his black hair off his shoulders. His pale blue eyes shone with fierce determination and his mouth was a firm, straight line. Just looking at him made everything inside her burn with a need that was nearly overwhelming. She wanted him. More than she'd ever wanted anything. Was she supposed to ignore that? Ignore the tug of something so fundamental?

God, she wished she knew what to do.

"I didn't ask for this, either," he said, his voice as soft and warm as the wind was cold. He stopped beside her and looked down into her eyes. "I'd long ago accepted that I would not have a Mate. Centuries since I've allowed a faint thought of finding the one woman meant for me to haunt me. To torment my dreams and fill too many solitary hours. But at last, I decided it was no way for a Guardian to live. How could I keep my mind on my duties if indulging in thoughts of a selfish need?

"No, I put the very idea of you aside, Emma, long ago. Now, when the notion of a Mate no longer even crosses my mind, you appear. A Campbell, no less." He laughed shortly and the sound tore at her. "Fate, I've learned, is at times, a vicious bitch."

"Well, that was flattering," she muttered, whipping her wind-driven hair back from her face. "Thanks very much."

"You feel the same and you know it, Emma." He shook his head. "Will you not admit at least that the Fates have played you as strange a hand as they have me?"

Reluctantly, she had to smile. "Okay, yes, I can admit that. I came here to take a few classes. To see Scotland. Demons and Guardians weren't exactly in the brochure."

"It's odd for you, I know. But," he added, "you've accepted it far better than most mortals would. It's the Scots blood in your veins. Makes you more open to the possibilities."

"It's Campbell blood," she reminded him.

He winced. "Aye, I know. But still Scots."

She smiled inwardly at the discomfort on his face. He really didn't like the Campbells. That would make his meeting her mother really entertaining. But, she told herself, that wasn't likely to happen, was it?

Shaking her head, Emma asked, "Bain, what does all of this mean for us?"

"It means we're meant."

He said it so easily, yet Emma knew he, too, was torn about this. She felt it in him. There was doubt in his mind and heart. There was concern for her—with the threat of Derek the Demon hanging over her head. And there was hesitation in him about changing the way he'd always lived his life. His duty to defend humans from demons was a huge part of him and she knew that he was wondering if he could do it as well as he always had if he allowed himself to care for her.

He was wondering, too, if perhaps the Fates hadn't made a big whopping mistake.

"You say that," she said, "but I'm picking up enough stray thoughts from you to know that you're not exactly thrilled with all of this."

He scowled at her as if he didn't like being reminded that she could read what he was thinking.

"Besides. We're meant? For what, Bain? For a lifetime?" She threw her hands up and her voice hitched a little higher. "Whose? Mine? Yours? You're immortal. I'm going to get old and die."

He reached for her, laid his big hands on her shoulders and pulled her in close. In spite of everything, Emma felt the heat of him flow into her body, easing away the chill in her blood. The cold in her soul. She snuggled in close to him, resting her head on his broad chest, listening to the steady thump of his heart, and she felt…*right*. As if she was exactly where she was supposed to be.

"There must be a way for us," he murmured, resting his chin on top of her head. "I will find it."

Emma wrapped her arms around his waist,

hung on and asked herself if she really wanted
him to find a way for them. God knew it would
be easier if she could simply walk away from
Scotland and pick up her old life. But she'd never
be able to do that. Not knowing that Bain existed.
Nothing was ever going to be easy or simple
again, she thought with a rueful smile.

Because, yes, she did want Bain to find a way
through this mess. A way for them to be together.
To claim whatever it was that linked them so
intricately together. It made no sense, of course.
But it was as if she'd known him forever. As if
she'd been born with these feelings for him and
had only been waiting for them to flower.

She knew his thoughts, how he felt. She saw
what kind of man he was. Who he was. And she
admired him. Wanted him. Cared for him.

But she couldn't say if she completely trusted
him.

He kept part of his mind closed to her.
Pieces of himself he denied her. Once they
made love—and she knew they would; it was
inevitable—would she be able to see all of those
hidden pockets inside him? Would she be able to
unravel the mystery of an ancient Highlander? Or
would he still find a way to keep himself separate
from her?

And a part of her wondered if she would be this drawn to him if she were still living in the dorm room at the university. If she were still going about her everyday life, would she be as intrigued by Bain? How could she be totally sure of anything? He'd swept her away from everything familiar and settled her down in a palace. Protected, perhaps, but cut off, with only him to lean on. How could she really know her own mind until life returned to normal? Until she could take a step back and look at everything objectively?

But what if that never happened? What if he kept her here indefinitely? It's not like she could escape him. Mr. Ancient Warrior was probably a pretty good tracker, too. He'd find her wherever she went. And so, undoubtedly, would the demon. So she was trapped here. Forced to trust Bain whether she was ready for that or not.

God, could her life get more confusing?

"Your mind is a jumble of thoughts," he said softly, lifting one hand to push a handful of red curls off her forehead.

"You shouldn't be peeking, anyway," she snapped, and hoped he hadn't been able to read any one thing in particular. People shouldn't be able to read each other's minds, she told herself. Thoughts were private and, sometimes, embarrassing. For example, the fantasies she'd been having the past couple of days all starred Bain Sinclair. Images raced through her mind, leaving her staggered even as he groaned.

"If you keep having thoughts like those, lass, I'll not promise to not look at them."

"Oh, great." She closed her eyes, mortified. When she looked up at him, he was smiling. "Just because my thoughts get a little X-rated now and then doesn't mean I'm ready to jump into the mating bed with you."

"Fine, then." He inclined his head with a regal nod. "The mating bed, as you call it, can wait. Tell me what troubles you."

"God," she said with a choked-off laugh. "Where to start? You said that finding your Destined Mate would make your strength, your powers, grow."

"Yes."

"Is that why you're keeping me here? To use me?"

"No."

She leaned back and looked up at him, but his face gave away nothing of what he was feeling. Emma tried to look into his mind, but he'd shuttered his thoughts from her. That told her one thing, at least. He didn't completely trust her, any more than she did him.

"That's it? Just *no?*"

He sighed and tossed his hair back from his face. "If my only reason for having you here was to use you, I'd have already bedded you, lass. Sex with you will give me increased strength. Whereas this constant torture of wanting and not having is only driving me around the bend."

"Torture?"

"You doubt it?" He pulled her closer and Emma felt the hard, thick length of him pressing into her abdomen. "My body aches for yours. As yours does for mine. You think to hide it from me, but your need pulls at me. Your fantasies are all too clear. Would you lie now and pretend otherwise?"

Her eyes closed on a wave of something hot and delicious. Just having his hard body pressed to hers made her damp and more than ready for him. Every cell in her body wanted him and it took every ounce of her strength to not give in.

"Of course I want you. I'd have to be dead not to," she told him. "But it doesn't change anything."

She pulled out of his arms, took a halting step back and tried to regain whatever pitiful sense of control over this situation she could. And while she waited for her heart to stop pounding, she waved one hand at the sword he still carried strapped to his hip. Deliberately, she changed the subject. "Did you find the demon?"

"No." His features slipped into a mask of frustration that, for once, had nothing to do with her. "The portal at the library is silent, and there were no trace energy patterns nearby. He's not come back yet."

"Yet?"

He nodded, his gaze fixed on her. "Yes. He will return. And I think I know why."

Judging by the look in his eyes, what he had to say wasn't going to make her happy. But Emma had to know. She'd already figured out that ignoring all of this wasn't going to make it go away. And until this situation with the demon was settled, then nothing else in her life would be, either.

She waited for him to speak, keeping her gaze locked with his.

"I spoke to Karras," Bain finally said, "the Guardian who lives here. He told me there was word of an archaeological find newly placed in Edinburgh University."

"What kind of find?" Apprehension roiled

inside her at his tone. This wasn't going to be good and she knew it.

Scowling, he pushed both hands through his shoulder-length hair and stared into her eyes as if he could somehow bolster her courage by sheer force of will. "It's a cup. Bronze, they say, etched with what my friend claims are demonic runes along with the clan name Campbell. The cup dates to ancient days. To before my time."

Before his time meant pre-eleventh century, Emma thought, amazed that she could actually *have* that thought without freaking out anymore. Demonic runes? What were they? And why the Campbell name? Oh, this couldn't be good.

Emma felt as though the ground beneath her feet was tipping and she was left to scramble to keep her footing. She took a breath and asked, "What does that have to do with the demon wanting *me?*"

He looked into her eyes and a shiver swept over her. She'd seen lots of things in his eyes in the past few days, but until that moment, Emma had never once seen even the slightest flicker of fear. But it was there now.

Fear for her.

"It's to do with how the cup is to be used,

Emma." He reached for her, but she skipped back, shaking her head.

"Oh, God." Emma swallowed hard. "I'm not going to like this, am I?"

He moved closer to her, and this time laid his big hands on her shoulders and let his body heat drain into hers. "The demon needs Campbell blood, Emma."

Bain paused, gritted his teeth until his jaw looked as tight as steel, then added, "He needs *your* blood."

Chapter 5

Her breath hitched in her chest.

Panic coiled in the pit of her stomach and immediately sprung loose, shooting bone-deep fear throughout her body. Even with Bain as close as he was, she felt cold right down to her soul. This was so much worse than she had thought.

Not just any Campbell? Me, specifically? God, why?

"Your mother," he said, answering the question she'd only whispered in her mind. "She's a descendant of those who first forged the cup."

"Oh, God." Her mind was racing, and even if Bain was reading her thoughts, she knew he wasn't getting much. There were too many images and emotions flashing through her brain for anything to make sense.

Emma struggled for air while fear clawed and chewed at her insides. The demon needed her blood. *Her* blood. All because of something that had happened more than a thousand years ago? How was that fair?

"Michael, the being in charge of the Guardians, checked into your history for me." Bain ran his powerful hands up and down her arms in a rhythmic motion designed to soothe. But she was beyond comfort, well into a panic zone that was so deep and so all-consuming she couldn't see a way out.

"My history?" she repeated.

"Your family's, that is," Bain corrected. "He sifted through the threads of time and found those tying you to the cup. Your mother's people once made a pact with a powerful demon. They were given the cup to use in…ceremonies."

"What kind of ceremony?"

His eyes met hers and held. "Blood rites."

"Sacrifices, you mean," she said, her voice as hollow as she felt. The chill sweeping over her was so deep that not even the heat of Bain's hands could dispel it. *Blood rites* was such a clean phrase, she thought, for something so ugly. "The ancient Campbells made sacrifices to a demon. For power?"

"Aye," he said, "and for land. Money."

She staggered back, tearing herself from his grip, covering her mouth with one hand as if she could bottle up the scream fighting to get past her throat. This was all too terrifying. Too real. "So what? The demon's been waiting for me to come here? If I'd never come to Scotland…"

"It would have found you eventually," Bain said, walking toward her with careful, easy steps as if he expected her to bolt. "And I wouldn't have been there to protect you. So it's better that it happened now. Here."

Maybe, but if she'd had anywhere to run to, Emma might have. But she didn't. She was alone in Scotland, but for Bain. The man standing between her and a demon who wanted her for—

"Why me?"

"You are the youngest of your bloodline," he explained. "It's how the curse was worded. The youngest of the clan retained the power."

"But I don't have any power," she argued

frantically. This had to be a mistake. How could decisions acted upon centuries ago, made by people she'd never heard of, have anything to do with her?

"Your blood does."

"Of course it does," Emma muttered. She shoved her hands through her hair and shook her head, as if by denying all of this she could make it go away. "What does he want my blood for?"

Again, Bain looked as though he'd rather do anything but answer her question. But he did, his voice low, reluctant. "He fills the cup with your blood, spills it onto the portal and it becomes an open gateway for eternity."

She swayed in place. "So he'd use me to destroy the world."

"Yes." He reached for her again, holding her tightly enough to help her stand beneath the burden of all this information. As if he knew her knees were wobbly and her head was spinning. But then, he probably did, Emma told herself. He could read her thoughts. Hear her terror. Feel her desperation.

"The demon would open a permanent gateway from his dimension into this one," he said, his voice a low rush of sound that seemed to reverberate deep inside her. "There would be no way to stop it. No way to halt their invasion. They would run riot over this world, its people, until they destroyed everything."

Vivid images of rampant destruction rose up in her mind in response to that statement and Emma wanted to run, but knew she couldn't. Because of the mindless stupidity of her ancestors, she was now the key to a demon's plot. How was she supposed to deal with this? "My blood does all that?"

"Aye." He pulled her closer, wrapping his strong arms around her and holding her with an iron grip that shut off her air and oddly comforted her at the same time. "But I will not let it happen. We will get the cup and destroy it before the demon has a chance to use it. Or you."

Emma nestled into his embrace, needing the comfort, the strength, he could give her. She felt adrift on some wildly rolling sea, with wave after wave crashing down over her as she struggled to breathe. Three days ago, her biggest problem had been picking out the right outfit to wear to her first pub. Now, she was the key to the destruction of the world.

"How?" She needed to know everything. "How do we destroy it?"

"Living flame," he murmured gently, his tone more soothing than his words. "A Guardian may stir the fires of eternity, but it's a dangerous task. One mistake and those flames will burn forever, endangering everyone. It's not a thing we do lightly."

Living flame. It even sounded dangerous.

"What happens then, Bain?" Her words were whispered against his chest, as if she were half-afraid to have him hear her. "If we stop the demon, what happens to us?"

"I have told you. We will find a way."

And what if there isn't a way?

Then we will take what we can while we can.

Speaking to him with her thoughts built an incredible intimacy she never would have believed possible. It was almost as if they were one person. Two halves coming together to become complete.

She looked up at him, into his now-so-familiar eyes and felt a rush of something hot and thick pouring through her. He was right.

For three days, she'd been here, living with him, avoiding him, ignoring the heat that lay between them. Why? Because she didn't completely trust him? Because she was afraid that they had no future? Because she was so far out of her element here that taking one more step might push her over the edge?

Yes to all three. Yet there was more, too. She was afraid that if she gave in to what she felt for him, she'd never be able to let him go and where would that leave her? But the bottom line was, whatever they shared was real. It was now. And wasn't denying it only punishing both of them?

Yes, his voice whispered in her mind, *a punishment neither of us deserves.*

She narrowed her gaze on him. Though it was sexy at times, knowing he could read her thoughts was still a bit unsettling. "Seriously? You've got to stop dipping into my mind whenever you feel like it. It's creepy."

"'Tis natural between mates. We can have no secrets from each other."

"Oh, there's the path to happiness," Emma said wryly.

"What do you fear?" he asked, stroking her cheek with one fingertip.

"The demon. Me. You. This. Everything." She stepped out of his embrace and instantly missed the feel of him pressed against her as she would have an arm or a leg. He was already so much a part of her, Emma didn't know how she would go on without him in her world. Yet, how could she stay in his?

"You fear me?"

Shaking her head, she looked up at him, stared into those ice blue eyes and said, "No," she corrected. "It's not really fear. It's... I don't even know."

"Three days I've given you to grow used to the fact that I am your Mate." His voice was a low growl. Naked desire was etched on his features. "You say you care for me, but you do not admit that we belong together. Three days I've wanted you. Ached for you. No more."

"Bain..."

No more.

That single thought roared through her mind as he grabbed her again, pulled her in close and kissed her as though his life depended on the touch of her mouth to his. And maybe, she thought wildly, it did.

Her body felt electrified. Visions swam in

and out of her mind, images of him wielding a sword in a soft, gray mist. Leading a charge of screaming Highlanders into battle. She saw him die and her heart ached for him, her soul crying out to save him. Then she saw him through centuries of solitude, fighting demon after demon.

She saw him at his home, a rugged stone castle high on a hill. And she saw him the night they met in the library with fear and horror standing between them. The night his gaze collided with hers and sent Emma's world spinning off its axis. She actually *felt* what he had when he realized she was his Mate. She felt the elation, the pride, the roaring hunger racing through his system, and she felt her own match it.

Closing her mind to everything but the feel of him, she gave herself up to the wonder of his touch. He did things to her no man had ever done. Made her want as she never had. Made her need more than anyone ever had.

"Ah, Emma," he whispered, tearing his mouth from hers to bury his face in the curve of her neck. "I've been in such pain the past few days, tell me you'll welcome me now."

"I will," she said, barely able to form the words.

Eyes wide open, she stared up at the leaden sky and only then realized they were on the patio, in complete view of anyone in the house who might glance out a window. "Not here, though."

"Aye. Here. Now." He straightened briefly, waved one hand and the air surrounding them rippled like the surface of a wind-blown lake. She reached out one hand, felt a barrier there and turned to look up at him. "This is what you did at the library that night."

"Aye," he said, reaching for her again, hunger flashing in his eyes. "Now we're invisible to the world outside this bubble."

She glanced at the house, then shifted her gaze back to his. It felt as if she'd known him always. He was the missing piece of her heart. Her soul. And for however long she would have him, Emma would savor it. Revel in what she found when they touched. What he made her feel when he looked at her as he was now.

He must have been reading her mind again, because in seconds, he'd stripped her out of her clothes and pulled his own off, as well. He was immense, her Highlander. Broad chest, heavy arms, with a Celtic cross tattooed on his right bicep. He tossed his black hair back over his shoulder and stood proudly naked, giving her time to look her fill. So she did. Flat stomach, bronzed skin, long, muscular legs and… Her eyes went wide and she felt the first flutter of nerves. "Um…"

I can see your thoughts, Emma. His laughter rippled through her mind along with his words. *Have no worries. We'll fit. We were meant.*

"Meant. Yes." She was meant for him. She knew it. Accepted it as a bone-deep knowledge that needed no proof. No explanation. Whatever else happened in her life, her world, this moment with Bain Sinclair was one she'd waited all through time for. Banishing that trickle of nerves, Emma threw her arms around his neck and held on tightly, sliding her palms up and down his back as he kissed her thoroughly. His lips and tongue drew gasps and moans from her.

He slid his hands over her body in a frantic dance of exploration as if he couldn't wait another moment to have her beneath him. Emma felt the same. Electric. Dazzled. Shaken. She needed him. Now.

Her body was hot, ready, and when he laid her on the cool, damp lawn, she shivered as the tender blades of grass caressed sensitized flesh. Then he was kneeling between her legs, his gaze locked on hers as he lifted her hips, positioning her body perfectly.

"You're a wonder, lass," he said, sliding his big hands up and down her thighs until she writhed with the need clamping down on her.

Emma held her breath and looked up into those amazing blue eyes of his. Fire flashed in their depths and she knew that his desire for her was quickening into an inferno. She felt his want rippling off of him in thick waves and felt her own body responding. She'd never known such immense hunger. It was as if she'd been starving all her life and then suddenly was offered a banquet.

"Come to me, Bain," she whispered, lifting her arms to welcome him, parting her thighs farther in invitation.

She kept her gaze fixed on him as he entered her with a swift rush of tenderness and strength. He had been right, of course. They fit. Beautifully. She felt her body stretching to accommodate him, even as she locked around him. Every last glorious inch of him claimed her in a way no man ever had before—and as no man ever would again.

Instantly, he set a rhythm she raced to follow. He bent his head to take first one of her nipples, then the other, into his mouth. His lips, teeth and tongue worked her sensitive flesh until she could hardly draw breath. There were too many sensations coursing through her at once, each of them demanding her attention.

And then there was nothing but him. The friction his body created with hers. No lingering foreplay and no need for it. The ache was all. The astonishing rush of sensation overpowering. He loomed over her, an ancient warrior, long black hair a curtain on either side of his face. His hard mouth was lush and glorious as he claimed a kiss while his body claimed everything else.

Again and again, he pushed her higher, faster, wilder than anything she could have expected. Emma's mind touched his. She felt his need as well as her own. Read his astonishment at what was happening between them. Saw herself through his eyes and felt his raging desire like a storm. She *felt* his pleasure as if it were her own and sensed that he was experiencing her own discordant thoughts and emotions.

When the first thundering crash of her climax

dropped on her, Emma screamed his name and locked her legs around his hips, holding him to her. Her body rocked beneath his as she rode the hard, fast currents of an orgasm that threatened to splinter her heart and mind. Then moments later, his body clenched as hers had and Emma experienced his soul-shattering release as completely as he did.

Bain felt the very foundations of his life shake beneath him. He'd had no idea that the connection between he and his Mate would be so all-encompassing. Bracing himself over her, his body still locked deeply within hers, he felt the connection they shared become as indestructible as bands of iron. Once-fragile bonds tightened like invisible coils, drawing them together, making them one.

He felt her heartbeat as his own. He looked into her mind and read the same stunning sense of wonder that had left him shaken. He felt her touch, her fingers on his face, as a blessing, a kind of miracle that he'd never known in all his long centuries of life.

His soul trembled. His heart opened and his eyes were seeing his world as if for the first time. All the long years of emptiness he'd survived were now no more substantial than autumn leaves, lost in a cold wind. Here was all. Here, he thought, looking down into green eyes shining with the wonder of what they had just experienced, was *everything*.

Cupping her face in the palm of one big hand, Bain looked deeply into her beautiful eyes and solemnly swore, "I will never let you go."

Chapter 6

Edinburgh by night was a magical place.

Lamplight glittered on rain-wet cobblestone streets. Laughter and music spilled out of pubs, drifted on the cool wind and floated along the streets, a pied piper's siren song to the young, or the lonely. Ancient buildings, some tipped weirdly as if leaning against each other for support, lined the roads and cars were parked half on and half off the sidewalks.

The narrow alleyways, or "closes" as they were called here, looked shadow filled, forbidding and every bit as haunted as the city tour guides insisted they were. Edinburgh Castle, once home to a doomed queen, sat atop a hill looking down on the city it had stood watch over for centuries. Moonlight shifted in and out of existence as the ever-present clouds chased one another across the sky.

Bain's footsteps were soundless and Emma tried to match him. But even in her tennis shoes, she managed to make noise. Alongside a man who moved with such stealthy confidence, Emma felt clumsy in comparison.

Her hand firmly in his, she felt his strength pouring into her and read the steely determination in his mind. She knew he'd wrapped them in an invisibility bubble again so that they could move through the darkened city undetected by humans. But still she felt as though there were unseen eyes watching them.

"Tell me again why we're doing this at night," she whispered, whipping her head around to stare down the long, empty street behind them.

He briefly squeezed her hand. "Because there'll be no one in the archives to gainsay us as we search for the cup."

"Right. Right." She knew that. And it made sense, of course. Even invisible, they couldn't really snatch an artifact, build a living flame and destroy it while there were people in the building.

Then she thought of something. "Can we do the flame thing while we're invisible?"

"No." One word. Harsh. Sharp. And Emma saw in Bain's thoughts he wasn't happy about that. "Maintaining both spells at once is difficult. I can't risk the flames spreading."

So they'd be out in the open where anyone could see them. Fabulous. But the archives would be empty and the demon wouldn't be there. Or maybe good old Derek would be hanging out in the library waiting for her return. That was never going to happen. Emma doubted she'd ever be able to go into any library ever again without ropes of garlic, a cross or two and maybe Bain's sword, just for good measure.

They are not vampires, Emma, Bain chided with a deep-throated chuckle. *Merely demons.*

Merely? There's nothing "merely" about demons, O great and powerful Highlander.

Thank you. He shot her a long look and a half smile. *It is good to know you see me as I am.*

Emma laughed, as he'd meant her to, and it felt good no matter how briefly it lasted. Honestly, she'd never been more aware. More alert.

Beside her, Emma's warrior moved with a deadly sort of grace that made her heart flutter and her hormones sit up and shout hallelujah despite how scared she was. Ever since they'd made love in the yard the day before, they'd scarcely been apart. Sex had never been like this before.

Every time they were together, their hearts, their souls, their minds became more intertwined. Now, it was as if she couldn't tell where she left off and Bain began. She was closer to him than she'd ever thought it possible to be to anyone and still…there was something he wasn't telling her. Something he kept locked behind a wall in his mind that she simply couldn't see past.

And that worried her.

He had full access to her thoughts. She felt him, a shadow in her mind, all the time. And now she wondered how she'd ever lived without that intimate touch. She knew he was aware of just how scared she was. How sad she was that she could see no future for them. How absolutely she loved him.

Yet despite her feelings, she'd yet to say the words. Even knowing that he could read them in her thoughts wasn't the same. If she said *I love you* and then had to walk away, Emma wasn't sure she'd be able to survive their separation. So she couldn't say it. Couldn't make that last commitment.

"You worry."

"You betcha," she said, shooting him a glance, then once more looking over her shoulder. The street was empty, lamplight shining like tiny globes of gold in the darkness, spreading pools of light across the damp cobblestones. Pins and needles scampered up and down her spine.

She could swear they were being watched.

"There is no need," he said, and stopped long enough to pull her close to him for a tight, one-armed hug. In his free hand, he held his sword, ready for battle. "I will protect you. We will find our way."

"I really do want to believe that," Emma said, staring up into those icy blue eyes that could hold her captivated with a glance.

"Then do."

She laughed shortly and huffed out a breath that ruffled the short, red curls on her forehead. "Okay. What was I thinking? I'll believe."

One corner of his mouth tipped up and Emma's body turned to liquid heat as erotic images flashed through her mind. Clearly, her body didn't care that they were in danger.

Instantly, Bain groaned low in his throat. "Guard your thoughts, Emma. You can't tempt me here. There are other things we must do."

"Me tempt you?" She smiled wryly. "Just looking at you makes me want to—" Another very explicit image rolled through her mind. *Her, straddling him, arching her back as he lifted his hands to cup her breasts. Her body encasing his, her hips grinding against him, taking him deeper, higher. Sweet friction as he moved within her. The sweeping sensations of a soul-shattering orgasm ripping through them both…*

"Enough!" He cupped the back of her head, pulled her close and kissed her, hard, long and deep. When he was through he pulled his head back and each of them fought for air. "Let us finish this and then I will show you *my* thoughts."

Emma trembled with the miniquakes she now recognized as foreplay shocks. Almost as good as the real thing, they rippled through her with tiny jolts of expectation that nearly made her forget they were on the trail of a cursed cup designed to hold her blood.

Nearly.

"Okay," she said, nodding as that thought went through her mind. "Back on track."

Without another word, he crossed the street, taking her with him, leading her toward the darkened university. A scant few windows shone with the soft glow of lamplight. Mostly, the blackened windowpanes of the school stood out as darker shadows in the gloom. Sort of like empty eyes staring into space. And over all, the hint of danger lay like a thick fog.

"Don't you feel it, too?" she asked, turning her head toward Bain.

"I do." His eyes glittered in the light and his features were shadowed, harsh. "There are demons near. They sense the energy barrier." His hand tightened on hers. "As I can see the trace energy signatures they leave behind, they can sense mine."

"So the invisibility thing is pretty much useless?" She glanced around, even more nervous than before. "That makes me feel better."

He squeezed her hand briefly. "The energy field is not a defense against demons. It's only to protect us from prying human eyes while we do what needs doing."

But there are no humans watching us. Emma's frantic gaze swept the darkness, searching in the shadows, even as she hoped she wouldn't see a thing. Knowing demons were out there, staring at her, was completely different from actually *seeing* them.

Her stomach jumped, her nerves seemed

to sizzle in warning. Suddenly, she felt those watching eyes even more fiercely than she had before. There was dark power out there and it was focused on them. Was it Derek watching them? Or a different demon? Or even worse, a *troop* of demons, all working together to kill Bain and her? And what if the demons didn't know where to go at all? Were they simply leading the demon threatening her to exactly what he needed?

"Bain—"

"I feel your fear," he said softly, gaze still moving over their surroundings, scanning, watchful for the slightest movement that might constitute a threat. "Don't allow it. If the demon follows, I'll dispatch it."

"So you're expecting Derek to show up." *Great. That makes me feel fabulous.*

"I always expect trouble," he countered. *That way I am rarely surprised.*

But Emma felt as if she'd been nothing but surprised for days now. She didn't know how much more adrenaline her body could take without just imploding.

Then the university loomed before them, the old buildings, constructed of gray stone, boasting mullioned windows, looked like an ancient fortress rather than a school. And, for some reason, that made Emma feel better. Maybe because the man she was with had come from before the time this place was built? Maybe because he belonged, not in a city but on the ramparts of a castle? If anyone could get them through the dangers of tonight, Emma knew it was her Highlander. Pride rushed through her in a wave almost strong enough to quash her terror.

"When this is finished, Emma," Bain promised, "I will take you from this crowded city and show you the Highlands. You will love it."

Emma looked at him and hoped he was right. Oh, she knew she'd love the Highlands. How could she not, with her very own Highlander to show her the country, to make her see it through his eyes? But what she didn't know was if she'd be alive to go with him. Even her pride and faith in Bain wasn't enough to convince her that she had a future past tonight. And should she live, how long would she have with Bain before she was forced to leave?

A scuffle of sound reached Emma and ended whatever she might have said to Bain. Before she could react, the world seemed to explode.

Stay down!

Bain's voice was harsh and loud and brooked no argument. Emma dropped to the cobblestones, their damp cold seeping into the knees of her jeans as she watched three demons rush Bain from the shadows. They were pale, their faces white as bone, their long arms ending in hands curled into claws. One of them howled and the sound seemed to echo up and down the street, sending shivers along Emma's spine. Her mouth went dry and everything inside her iced over. Fear was a living, breathing entity within her. She felt helpless and didn't like it.

She never heard Derek approaching from behind her until it was too late.

He snaked one hand around her mouth, and with the other grabbed her hair and viciously yanked her head back. Naked throat arched toward the sky, she sent one quick mental scream.

Bain!

She caught only a glimpse of her Highlander's furious eyes when he whirled to see Derek with his hands on her. Then the other three demons pounced on Bain as Derek carried her off toward the university…and the waiting Campbell Cup.

Bain was filled with a fury that nearly choked him. Roaring his rage, he tore through the demons he now realized had been sent to distract him. It had worked. He'd been so focused on protecting Emma from this, he hadn't sensed the *real* attack coming from another direction. Derek had used Bain's own concern for Emma against him and Bain had fallen for it. That only infuriated him further. It was *his* fault Emma was now in danger. *His* mistake that had put her in danger. Now all he could do was end this battle and get to her as quickly as possible.

Derek would use Emma to open the portal and keep it open. Preventing that from happening should be the most important thing to him and yet, after a thousand years of protecting humanity, Bain realized he didn't care about the damned portal. If it was opened and he was forced to stand guard over it for eternity, he would. Battling one after the next, every demon hell spat out at him.

The portal was unimportant. The only thing he worried about now was Emma's safety.

Once that doorway was open, Derek would have no further use for her.

She would die.

Unless Bain prevented it.

With single-minded determination, Bain emptied everything he had into the fight with the three demons. His blade sang as he swung it with fierce abandon. His muscles bunched and cries of agony filled the still night air. A demon claw raked along Bain's arm and blood flowed freely. He didn't notice. Another of the demons kicked out at his legs and Bain leaped into the air, avoiding that pitiful attempt to bring him down.

Again and again, he squared off against the three, his body moving in long familiar moves even as his mind sought Emma's. But her thoughts were closed to him. Was she too afraid? Was she unconscious? There was another explanation, but Bain refused to accept that. She wasn't dead. Not yet, anyway. Derek had need of her and so would keep her alive. For now.

That thought gave him the impetus to finish the fight in a few blindingly fast moves. First one, then another, then finally the third demon succumbed to his blade until all three opponents were writhing on the street, wet cobblestones shining black with the stain of demon blood.

"You're too late, Guardian," one of them managed to say, its words coming garbled from a mouth sliced open by Bain's sword. "We have the woman and the gates will open."

He paid them no heed. They were merely the

distraction and he wouldn't be drawn away from his objective.

"She dies tonight," another one promised, grunting as Bain gave it a kick that sent it sprawling into one of its brothers.

"You lose!" the first crowed, then moaned, clapping one hand to its ruined face.

"We shall see," Bain muttered, draping the three demons in the finely meshed, silver Guardian netting. The harder they struggled against the net's hold, the tighter they would be caught. The perfect trap to keep them detained and unable to hurt anyone else. Bain stood, grabbed his sword, then waved his free hand across the demons, wrapping them in an energy field that would hide their presence from all but him.

When he was finished, he spun, faced the hulking black shadow of the university and raced toward the woman who was now the center of his life.

Chapter 7

"You stupid bitch." Derek yanked at her hair until Emma's eyes watered. "You won't stop this."

He forced her through one of the oldest buildings on the Edinburgh campus, using her like a divining rod. He faced her first one way and then the next, down long, empty corridors of what seemed to be an ancient section of the university. When he didn't find what he was searching for, he dragged her farther along the darkened halls.

Now that her time was running out, all Emma wanted was the chance to tell Bain she loved him. To let him know that the past week—despite everything—had been the most amazing of her life. That she would love him forever. That maybe, one day, she'd be born again and they'd have another chance.

But even with that, she kept her thoughts closed to him, afraid of distracting him while he was fighting. He would come to her. She knew it. *Believed* it. All she had to do was stay alive long enough for him to come storming to her rescue.

Then her racing thoughts crashed to an end. She jolted in Derek's grip as something dark and ancient awakened in her blood and made it buzz as if it sizzled just beneath her skin. Evil wasn't just a word, she told herself as she felt the black stain of it slide through her system. It was alive and hungry and calling to her as if to a lover. Emma moaned and pulled back, instinctively trying to distance herself from the source of that power.

Derek laughed in her ear and his voice was a hiss of sound. "I knew you'd find it for me. Blood calls to the cup. Soon this will be over. Soon, my brothers will own this world and all of you will service us."

Oh, God.

Fist still in her hair, Derek dragged her down the hall, enjoying her struggles to get free. The dark heat emanating from the cup was more intense the closer they got and Emma's body erupted in a sheen of sweat. She couldn't breathe. Couldn't force enough air into her lungs to keep from feeling light-headed, dizzy and disoriented.

At last, her mind helplessly sought out Bain's. *It's here. Derek found it. Help me.*

Emma!

The roar of her Highlander's voice in her mind was a momentary comfort. Finally, though, Emma's body seized up at her nearness to the cup. A faint, tight moan slid from her throat and Derek laughed. Throwing the closest door open, he stepped inside and spotted the very thing he was searching for.

Emma dropped to the floor, trying to make herself a smaller target. She curled into herself, trying to ease the racking pains shuddering through her now that she was so close to that damned cup.

It was no use, though. Just being in the same room with the thing was killing her. She felt her bones shrieking. Felt her soul cringe and her blood boil. There was ancient power in that cup. Dark and evil.

She looked up as Derek took the cup from a low shelf and ran his long, pale fingers over it in slow, loving strokes. The ancient bronze cup was battered and stained, its once-pristine surface blackened through time and the evil that had brought it into existence. The inscription etched around its rim was barely legible. But when Derek lifted it, those faded symbols suddenly illuminated with a dark red light that seemed to burn into the bronze, rejuvenating the cup into what it had been in the beginning.

A dark promise of death and power and change.

"You see?" Derek sighed. "It reacts to me. It knows its time has come."

Emma watched him smile at the damn thing, and for a moment, she half expected him to kiss it as sports champions kissed a hard-won trophy.

He slanted a look at her. "The demon world has long sought this cup. Forged by your ancestors for use when worshiping the old ones."

He walked close and crouched beside her where she huddled on the floor. His burning, maniacal gaze speared into her eyes. "It was lost centuries ago. Even my kind couldn't find it.

Buried and forgotten, the cup lay hidden beneath the earth. Until a new housing project was begun. It was freed from the muck and brought here to wait for your arrival. Now it sings to me."

Pain welled and blossomed inside her. The closer the cup was to her, the deeper the agony twisting within. How could her ancestors have forged a bargain with whatever had created that cup? How could they have thought, even for a moment, that anything was worth the fetid stench of the thing being brought into this world?

She shuddered, lungs collapsing, brain burning, and still she managed to look into Derek's eyes and whisper, "Bain will stop you."

"That's where you're wrong, bitch." He smiled. "Your Guardian is as good as dead."

"Not quite yet."

Emma heard Bain's voice and reacted instantly. Fighting the crippling pain inside her, she took advantage of Derek's momentary surprise. She reached out, batted the cup out of his hand, then watched as it rolled across the room toward Bain. He kicked it out of reach, lifted his sword and smiled at the demon. "Your plan is finished."

Her hand burned where she'd touched the cup, but already, with distance, the pain she felt began to fade just enough to make drawing breath easier.

"I'll kill the bitch!" Derek dragged her to her feet, and stood behind her, using her body as a shield. He grinned at Bain and said, "So you see, your plan ends, as well, Guardian."

Before Emma could figure out what Derek meant by that, he bit her.

She screamed while white-hot pain lanced through her throat as his teeth dug deeply into her flesh. This, she thought wildly, she hadn't expected. Her eyes met Bain's horrified gaze and she felt agony spiral through her system like a tightly wound string suddenly released. Heat, then cold, washed over her, *in* her, as if something hideous—something alive—was racing through her bloodstream. Her gaze locked on Bain, she saw fear dazzle his eyes before the edge of her vision began to go gray.

Over, she thought. *All over now with no hope of a happily ever after.*

A shout of pain, raw with rage, tore from Bain's throat as he watched Emma slide slowly to the floor at the demon's feet. He heard her last coherent thought and his soul wept for her even as his body and mind raged with the need for vengeance.

Her green eyes were glazed, her already fair skin going pale as milk. Blood stained her torn throat and ran in bright rivulets down the front of her blue T-shirt. His heart shattered, Bain felt her agony as his own, took the pain inside him and used it to finish the demon that had brought all of this down on them.

Cup forgotten, the demon laughed. "You can't kill me on this plane, Guardian, but I've killed what's yours."

Bain had no time for conversation and no wish to talk to the smiling beast standing over Emma. Instead, Bain rushed him, lifted his sword and swung it in a wide arc. The razor-sharp blade sliced through Derek's neck in one clean stroke. The demon dropped to the floor and Bain kicked the body away from Emma.

Weakly, Emma clapped one hand to her neck. "Thought you said they couldn't be killed."

Bain spared the body a quick look. "It's not dead. Like a lizard, it will regenerate whatever it needs."

"That's…gross." She let her hand fall to her lap, glanced at the bright red blood coating her fingers, took a breath and said, "Not vampires, huh?"

Stop talking. He tore his shirt off, ripped at

the fabric, then folded a strip of the material into a thick square and used it as a pad, holding it to her injured neck. Too much blood loss, he thought, even knowing that the blood wasn't the real problem. There was no way to keep the truth from her. *You have been poisoned.*

"Poisoned? Great. How long do I have?" Her eyes held his, demanding truth when he would have preferred a more gentle lie.

His heart twisted in his chest. The love of his life was so near death it terrified him. He, a Guardian who hadn't known the bitter taste of fear in too many centuries to count, now felt it overwhelm him.

"Tell me, Bain," she insisted in a voice that was barely more than a hush.

"Not long." Fresh fear as well as despair jolted through Bain. He was going to lose Emma permanently unless he acted. Soon. But the "cure" was not a sure thing. How could he risk it? Yet how could he not?

I love you, you know.

Her voice sounded in his mind and he wondered frantically how he could go on throughout eternity never knowing the touch of her thoughts again.

"I know," he said, kissing her forehead, sweeping her curls back from her pale face.

She laughed shortly, painfully. *Not the response I wanted.*

"Then I will give you what you need to hear. What I need most desperately to say. I love you, Emma Campbell Madison," he told her softly. "And trust me when I say I never thought to put the words *love* and *Campbell* in the same sentence."

She smiled, as he'd hoped she would, then closed her eyes on a soft moan. Time was ticking past. Every moment lost brought them that much closer to an end that he could not even contemplate. How could he be expected to go on through the eons without Emma at his side? Without her smile, her laugh, her touch? How could he face a long eternity of darkness with no promise of love or laughter to warm him?

He could not. *Would not.* Bain knew he had to act quickly. But first, he must tell her what he was thinking and then convince her to take the risk. To chance life. With him.

There is a way to perhaps defeat the poison.

She slowly, painfully, opened her eyes and looked at him, waiting for whatever else came next.

"Living flame." He said the words aloud, as if testing the sound of them on his tongue.

Clearly confused, she frowned and asked, "How?"

"You must walk through it." She blinked at him and he heard her thoughts, scattershot through her mind. More than that, he felt her fear, her reluctance to leave him, and he felt her waning strength. He waited, though, for her to speak her doubts aloud.

"Through eternal fire?"

"Yes," he said, pulling her to her feet, supporting her weight easily when her knees buckled and she slumped against him. He cradled her tightly to his chest and knew that he would do whatever was necessary to keep her there. With him. Where she belonged. "It is dangerous. But it should work."

"Should?"

She was even paler now, her skin nearly translucent, as if she were already beginning to leave him and this world behind. Everything in Bain was a defiant fist, refusing to let her go.

He cupped her face in his palm, forcing her to look up into his eyes. "Hear me, Emma. There are no guarantees in life. Not even when one is immortal. Yes, there is a risk to you. The flames could kill you. But without them, you will most surely die and I find I can't bear the thought of it."

Her eyes shone with unshed tears and she tried to lift a hand to touch his face. But she couldn't quite manage the task. "You do love me."

"Aye," he muttered thickly, "I do at that and seeing you in pain is tearing at me. I won't lose you, Emma. But, ultimately, you are the one who must choose. Choose life, Emma. Choose the risk. If the eternal flames don't kill you, the poison will be gone from your system and you will be immortal."

Just like that?

He caught the flicker of hope in her mind and clung to it.

"Standing in the fire is not an easy thing," he warned. "The flames will consume the poison. Consume that damned cup. Consume your mortality."

"What'll be left?" Her voice was barely a whisper now, as if she were nearly too far gone already for him to reach.

"You," he insisted. "You will be left. The essence of you. And you will be with me. Always. There will be *us*. It will work, Emma. I will stand in the fire with you. I will take as much of the pain as I can, but you will have to trust me, Emma. Do you?"

Instead of answering, a question simmered in her mind and slammed into his.

You've been hiding something from me, Bain. Something in your mind you don't want me to see. So before I answer your question, tell me what that is.

His arms, so strong, so capable, felt useless as he cradled the only important thing in his world. He sensed her body shutting down, the demon's poison slithering through her blood, infecting tissue and bone. Draining the life from her inch by inexorable inch. All Bain knew was that she must survive, so he gave her the one thing he'd kept from her.

"I didn't want you to know that an immortal may give up eternity. Become human."

"What?" Her eyes were clouded now, nearly opaque as her eyesight failed. Her breath was coming in short, irregular gasps. "You could become human?"

"Yes," he said, ashamed now that he'd ever thought to hide it from her. "Guardians can choose to give up the life of battle, become mortal like their mates. But I didn't wish to. A warrior is all I have ever been. I could not step away from my duty, Emma. Not even for you."

You big dummy.

His eyebrows arched high on his forehead.

She sighed heavily. "I wouldn't want you to be less than you are, Bain. I fell in love with my Highland warrior. Why would I want him to be anything else?"

"I am a fool."

Yeah, pretty much. Her laughter was fading now, too, the soft sigh of it in his mind more of an echo of what it had once been.

"We can't wait," he announced. "The demon's poison spread faster than I expected."

Her head lolled against his chest. *I trust you, Bain. Build me a fire.*

He did. Holding her propped against him with one arm, with his free hand, he sketched ancient symbols in the air. His fingers drew light and magic from the cold, drafty room, and as he whispered words of an ancient tongue known only to the Guardians, the very air around them shimmered and twisted with power.

It seemed to Bain that it took forever to make the magic happen. The urge for speed crouched in his chest and howled at him to hurry up. The sane corner of his mind warned that one misspoken word could turn living flame on the world and create as much destruction as a demon's incursion. He could afford no mistakes—not only for what it might cost the human world, but for the reason that he would not have the time to cast this spell again. If he didn't get it right the first time, he would lose the woman who was everything to him.

The spell for eternal fire was a difficult one and his worry for Emma made it that much harder to concentrate. Still, he focused his energies, drawing on centuries of life and power to do what he must. This was the only chance she had. The only chance *they* had.

Emma felt a magical wind tousle her hair, then she opened her eyes to watch her Highlander. He looked too good to be true, she thought, a weary smile lifting one corner of her mouth. She wanted another hour with him. Another night. An eternity.

She couldn't bear to lose him just when she'd found him. But she was so tired. So empty. Her bones were mush. Her strength was nearly gone. She listened to the steady, hard beat of Bain's heart beneath her ear and told herself that it wasn't such a bad way to die. In the arms of the only man she would ever love.

Hold tight to me, Emma! His thoughts crashed into her mind, allowing her no chance to slip away. He simply refused to accept her surrender to death. *There will be no leaving me, do you understand? Turn from the abyss tempting you. Return to me, Emma, and stand beside me as you were meant.*

Then light erupted into the darkness.

Emma forced her eyes open as magic electrically charged the air in the room. Shadows danced on the walls and heat licked at them as an inferno roared into life. Dazed, she stared at the wall of living fire in front of her. The flames danced and twisted and writhed against one another. Colors burst from the heart of the blaze—orange, blue, red, green, yellow.

It really *was* alive, she thought, and the heat was its heartbeat.

All around them, the shadows slipped away, unable to stand against the vivid brightness of a light so otherworldly. The Campbell Cup, so long coveted by the demon races, skittered noisily across the floor, as if drawn by the very heat of its destroyer. It was swept into the flames and was obliterated in an instant.

Oh, my God.

He must have heard the fear in her voice. He

looked into her eyes and whispered, "The fire vanquishes evil, Emma. There's nothing evil about you. You *will* be saved. I will allow nothing less, do you understand? I love you. Through all time, I will love you."

Emma smiled despite the weakness dragging at her and said softly, "Just don't let go of me, okay?"

Never. His promise echoed in her mind as he walked her into the heart of the firestorm.

Heat ripped through her and Emma gasped, throwing her head back, expecting to feel the excruciating pain of being burned alive. She stared into Bain's eyes and felt him with her. His heart, his soul, were so entwined with hers, it was impossible to feel the fear that should have been racking her.

Their hands met, palm to palm, and fingers locked. They stood, two halves of one whole, in the center of a fire that blew hot with the breath of eternity.

Heat, incredible heat, flashed through her veins and Emma felt the poison bleed from her cells, her muscles, her bones. As the flames danced around them, snapping, hissing, twisting around their limbs, tangling in their hair, all traces of the demon's venomous bite were consumed, leaving Emma alive in a way she never had been before. Her body awakened. Her soul swelled, blossoming with the promise of eternity, and as she stared into Bain's eyes and watched him smile, she knew.

It had worked.

Their desperate gamble had given them forever.

He pulled her close, murmured words both ancient and beautiful, and in the space of a single heartbeat the flames disappeared, winked out of existence. As if they had never been.

"It's over," she whispered, tipping her head back to grin at him in the sudden stillness. "I feel...different."

"As you should," he told her. "You're an immortal now, Emma. Just like me."

Immortal. The word sang through Emma's system, and for just a moment, she enjoyed the thrill of having eternity stretching out in front of her. She imagined watching the world change around her and always being able to reach out and touch the hand of the man who had saved her life—and that made that life worth living.

As you did for me, Emma, his mind whispered into hers. *For centuries, I was a man alone, and now, there is you. A priceless gift to one such as me.*

She smiled up at him, cupping his face between her palms. "I'll remind you of that the next time you're furious with me."

"I know you will, lass," he said, turning his face to kiss her palm. "What a fine time we'll have."

They would, Emma thought, since she now had an eternity to be with the man she loved more than anything. Then, she realized there were one or two things that had to be said. She poked him in the chest with her index finger.

"No more secrets, okay?"

"Agreed." He kissed her, nearly shattering her train of thought.

"And I'm going to finish school. Get my degree."

"If you wish."

"That means staying in the city during the school year, Mr. I-Can't-Wait-to-Get-Back-to-the-Highlands."

He frowned, but nodded, stroking her hair back from her face with gentle fingers. "I will find a Guardian to keep watch at my home until we return from this blasted city."

Emma wrapped her arms around his neck

and went up on her toes. "*And* you have to come home with me to meet my family."

His scowl deepened and she laughed.

"I see nothing funny about this," he told her as his arms came around her, holding her close.

"I know." Emma gave him a quick, hard kiss, then grinned again. "Oh, I think my mom's going to love you. But I warn you, my dad can be pretty protective."

"As a man should over his children."

"My brother will probably want to come back to Scotland for a visit with us."

"Aye," he muttered, rolling his eyes. "They're all welcome in our home, Emma. For as long as any of you like."

"I knew you'd say that," she said, still smiling. "You're a softy, Bain Sinclair."

He pulled her in tightly to him as if to dissuade her of that notion entirely.

Her eyebrows lifted as she pressed closer, rubbing her hips against his. "Okay, not a softy."

He bent his head to kiss her but she stopped him with one finger over his lips. "There's one more thing. You do realize, that for the rest of our eternal lives together, I'm never going to let you forget that I walked through fire for you."

"Leave it to a Campbell to find a way to torment me." He smiled at her and Emma's body went into overdrive.

She ran one hand across his bare, muscled chest until he shivered with the desire claiming them both. "Let's go home, Highlander, and I'll let *you* torment *me* for a while."

"I willna ever let you go, Emma. I doona think I could bear eternity wi' out ye."

A delighted laugh shot from Emma's throat as Bain gave her the Highland dialect she'd expected when she first met him—that seemed like a lifetime ago. And when he swept her into his arms and kissed her, she knew that an eternity spent with this man wouldn't be nearly long enough.

* * * * *

nocturne™

COMING NEXT MONTH

Available July 26, 2011

#117 ASHES OF ANGELS
Of Angels and Demons
Michele Hauf

#118 GUARDIAN WOLF
Alpha Force
Linda O. Johnston

REQUEST YOUR FREE BOOKS!

2 FREE NOVELS FROM THE PARANORMAL ROMANCE COLLECTION PLUS 2 FREE GIFTS!

YES! Please send me 2 FREE novels from the Paranormal Romance Collection and my 2 FREE gifts (gifts are worth about $10). After receiving them, if I don't wish to receive any more books, I can return the shipping statement marked "cancel." If I don't cancel, I will receive 4 brand-new novels every month and be billed just $21.42 in the U.S. or $23.46 in Canada. That's a saving of at least 21% off the cover price of all 4 books. It's quite a bargain! Shipping and handling is just 50¢ per book in the U.S. and 75¢ per book in Canada.* I understand that accepting the 2 free books and gifts places me under no obligation to buy anything. I can always return a shipment and cancel at any time. Even if I never buy another book, the two free books and gifts are mine to keep forever.

237/337 HDN FEL2

Name _____ (PLEASE PRINT)

Address _____ Apt. #

City _____ State/Prov. _____ Zip/Postal Code

Signature (if under 18, a parent or guardian must sign)

Mail to the **Reader Service:**
IN U.S.A.: P.O. Box 1867, Buffalo, NY 14240-1867
IN CANADA: P.O. Box 609, Fort Erie, Ontario L2A 5X3

Not valid for current subscribers to the Paranormal Romance Collection or Harlequin® Nocturne™ books.

Want to try two free books from another line?
Call 1-800-873-8635 or visit www.ReaderService.com.

* Terms and prices subject to change without notice. Prices do not include applicable taxes. Sales tax applicable in N.Y. Canadian residents will be charged applicable taxes. Offer not valid in Quebec. This offer is limited to one order per household. All orders subject to credit approval. Credit or debit balances in a customer's account(s) may be offset by any other outstanding balance owed by or to the customer. Please allow 4 to 6 weeks for delivery. Offer available while quantities last.

Your Privacy—The Reader Service is committed to protecting your privacy. Our Privacy Policy is available online at www.ReaderService.com or upon request from the Reader Service.

We make a portion of our mailing list available to reputable third parties that offer products we believe may interest you. If you prefer that we not exchange your name with third parties, or if you wish to clarify or modify your communication preferences, please visit us at www.ReaderService.com/consumerschoice or write to us at Reader Service Preference Service, P.O. Box 9062, Buffalo, NY 14269. Include your complete name and address.

PARA11

*Once bitten, twice shy. That's Gabby Wade's motto—
especially when it comes to Adamson men.
And the moment she meets Jon Adamson her theory
is confirmed. But with each encounter a little something
sparks between them, making her wonder if she's been
too hasty to dismiss this one!*

*Enjoy this sneak peek from ONE GOOD REASON
by Sarah Mayberry, available August 2011
from Harlequin® Superromance®.*

Gabby Wade's heartbeat thumped in her ears as she marched
to her office. She wanted to pretend it was because of her
brisk pace returning from the file room, but she wasn't that
good a liar.

Her heart was beating like a tom-tom because Jon Adamson had touched her. In a very male, very possessive way.
She could still feel the heat of his big hand burning through
the seat of her khakis as he'd steadied her on the ladder.

It had taken every ounce of self-control to tell him to
unhand her. What she'd really wanted was to grab him by
his shirt and, well, explore all those urges his touch had
instantly brought to life.

While she might not like him, she was wise enough to
understand that it wasn't always about liking the other person. Sometimes it was about pure animal attraction.

Refusing to think about it, she turned to work. When
she'd typed in the wrong figures three times, Gabby admitted she was too tired and too distracted. Time to call it a
day.

As she was leaving, she spied Jon at his workbench in
the shop. His head was propped on his hand as he studied
blueprints. It wasn't until she got closer that she saw his

eyes were shut.

He looked oddly boyish. There was something innocent and unguarded in his expression. She felt a weakening in her resistance to him.

"Jon." She put her hand on his shoulder, intending to shake him awake. Instead, it rested there like a caress.

His eyes snapped open.

"You were asleep."

"No, I was, uh, visualizing something on this design." He gestured to the blueprint in front of him then rubbed his eyes.

That gesture dealt a bigger blow to her resistance. She realized it wasn't only animal attraction pulling them together. She took a step backward as if to get away from the knowledge.

She cleared her throat. "I'm heading off now."

He gave her a smile, and she could see his exhaustion.

"Yeah, I should, too." He stood and stretched. The hem of his T-shirt rose as he arched his back and she caught a flash of hard male belly. She looked away, but it was too late. Her mind had committed the image to permanent memory.

And suddenly she knew, for good or bad, she'd never look at Jon the same way again.

Find out what happens next in ONE GOOD REASON, available August 2011 from Harlequin® Superromance®!

USA TODAY *bestselling author*

Lynne Graham

introduces her new Epic Duet

THE VOLAKIS VOW

A marriage made of secrets…

Tally Spencer, an ordinary girl with no experience of relationships… Sander Volakis, an impossibly rich and handsome Greek entrepreneur. Sander is expecting to love her and leave her, but for Tally this is love at first sight. Little does he know that Tally is expecting his baby…and blackmailing him to marry her!

PART ONE:
THE MARRIAGE BETRAYAL
Available August 2011

PART TWO:
BRIDE FOR REAL
Available September 2011

Available only from Harlequin Presents®.

SPECIAL EDITION

Life, Love, Family and Top Authors!

IN AUGUST, HARLEQUIN SPECIAL EDITION FEATURES
USA TODAY BESTSELLING AUTHORS
MARIE FERRARELLA AND *ALLISON LEIGH*.

THE BABY WORE A BADGE
BY *MARIE FERRARELLA*

The second title in the **Montana Mavericks:
The Texans Are Coming!** miniseries....

Suddenly single father Jake Castro has his hands full with
the baby he never expected—and with a beautiful young
woman too wise for her years.

COURTNEY'S BABY PLAN
BY *ALLISON LEIGH*

The third title in the **Return to the Double C** miniseries....

Tired of waiting for Mr. Right, nurse Courtney Clay takes
matters into her own hands to create the family she's
always wanted— but her surly patient may just be
the Mr. Right she's been searching for all along.

**Look for these titles and others in August 2011
from Harlequin Special Edition wherever books are sold.**

BIG SKY BRIDE, BE MINE! *(Northridge Nuptials)* by *VICTORIA PADE*
THE MOMMY MIRACLE by *LILIAN DARCY*
THE MOGUL'S MAYBE MARRIAGE by *MINDY KLASKY*
LIAM'S PERFECT WOMAN by *BETH KERY*